ENVY

Printed in the United States of America

Keen Vision Publishing, LLC

www.publishwithkvp.com

ISBN: 979-8-9992130-7-5

ENVY

BOSS BITCH CHRONICLES: VOLUME ONE

INFAMOUS BROWN

PROLOGUE

B*oss Bitch.* A lot of these chicks don't know the meaning of the title I hold for myself. These lames believe getting a nigga to take care of them is what put them in Boss Bitch status. Wrong!

A true Boss Bitch, like me, maneuvers and makes moves to make her own money. She controls money, demands money, and commands money. A Boss Bitch makes it her business to know how to make money work for her, not work for her money.

Being of Jamaican/Dominican descent, heritage, and breed, my first lessons were on family, loyalty, respect, and, of course, money. Papi and Momma made sure I knew the difference between being a boss and being an employee. Papi, being Dominican, taught me the values of being a successful and loved boss, while Momma, being Jamaican, taught me the values of being well respected, whether by fear or by love. They both taught me how to gain true loyalty, though as long as it was about money, I didn't care about loyalty from everyone.

Now, I wish I actually listened to that lesson.

Being born and raised in Memphis, TN, growing up in the Oakhaven neighborhood, that one lesson could have saved me from the betrayal of my so-called "sistahs." Me being gullible to the snakes. Though I should have known better, I got bit and poisoned.

I thought that I had some ride-or-die bitches on my side and found out that these hoes are as scandalous as a pimp gone legit at a women's church convention.

Now, here I sit in 201, fighting a case that should have been a clean getaway.

For those who don't know, 201 is Memphis County Jail, as in 201 Polar. Shelby fucking county! MCI!

These hoes ain't seen the last of me, though. When you good to the game, the game is good to you. I been good to the game, so rest assured, I'll be back shitting on these bitches harder than ever when I tough down.

My apologies, though. Where are my manners? Let me introduce myself. My name is Envy Sinclaire Santiago, and yes, Envy is my real name. Momma said she gave me my name because she knew there would be a lot of jealousy and envy shown towards me for various reasons.

Damn! Was she ever right!

Now, playing with the cards I've been dealt, it's time to elevate my game. I already have the pieces to the puzzle. I once stripped and sold my precious treasure, but now I'm what you call a "Madame." I got hoes and niggas under my employ. The difference between me and the rest is I don't have to gorilla nothing. Finesse has been my game forever. Conversation rules the nation, and persuasion is amazing.

I make more money in a month than some see in a year. My account reflects that even after I pay my bills and salaries. While these bitches are stuck in neutral, I'm steady switching gears like a NASCAR driver on one hundred miles straight away with no red line or engine failure.

So, the little setback I endured for a bullshit murder charge, yeah, I said little setback and murder charge in the same sentence, it's nothing that can really stop me. Don't believe me, just pay attention.

CHAPTER ONE

Spring 2017

Sitting in my cell, listening to the noise of the other chicks, I thought back on the news my lawyer gave me earlier today.

"Well, you should be out in a few days." Timberly Davis, my lawyer, said, "So sit back and expect to hear your name to be called for release."

A smile broke out across my lips.

Staring at the ceiling, I planned my next moves like a master chess player. One move that had to be made was relocation. I've lived in my neighborhood since my birth, but it was time to change my surroundings and switch scenes. Business and pleasure.

There was a thump at the end of my bunk, which meant only one of the two things. One, it was Jazmine or two, it was trouble. I lifted my head, hoping for the best and preparing for the worst.

"Damn, bitch! You gon' lay up all day, or are you gon' fuck with a bitch today?!" Jazmine asked from the end of my bunk.

Out of all the bitches I met since I got here, Jazmine was the most down-to-earth and the realest. When some bitches out of North Memphis wanted to click on me, Jazmine stepped up beside me. Come to find out, she was from North Memphis, known and well respected by many for the work she put in through the hood. So, when she stepped up, they backed down.

I was still cautious of her 'cause that was how setups happened. You got a group of girls to run up on an unsuspecting victim. One would come to the rescue and befriend the unsuspecting victim—only for the victim to learn what they want to know and leave a bitch needing an escort to the infirmary and your family on the target list.

Jazmine surprised me, though. It was her lawyer that got my case thrown out.

"Bitch! Ever since Timberly hollered at me, I been formulating a master plan for when I get out." I responded, getting up from my bunk. "And best believe I got something for you, too, girl!"

"I told you Timberly was the best, and she don't charge an arm and a leg!" Jazmine said, sitting on my bunk.

Jazmine was what you would call "model fine." She was 5'9" with a petite frame with enough ass, thighs, and breasts that she looked thicker than she was. Her caramel-brown skin was smooth and covered with tattoos in different places. You can tell she straight hood, no mistaking it.

Me, the exact opposite. I was 5'3" with a thick frame. My golden-brown skin showed the exotic blend of my Jamaican Dominican mix. My brownish-red hair reached halfway down my back; however, the envy of my look was completed by hazel green eyes and naturally long lashes. If I was darker, I would be a spitting image of my mom.

"Envy. Check it out." Jazmine said, getting up off of my bunk. "You keep saying you got me, but look. If you do, cool. Just know you don't owe me shit, so don't think or even feel obligated because we doing time together. Do what you got to do for you. I still get to have Timberly break my case open and get me off."

"Bitch, I ain't hearing that right now!" I interrupted her. "When I put my stamp on something, it becomes law and written in stone. You got my number already, so use it and use it well. Shit, if it's something I can do to help your case, have Timberly call me, or you call me."

Looking at Jazmine's face, I could see the skepticism in her eyes. I knew that when I showed her the real when the time came, she would know that when a Boss Bitch speaks, there's nothing to doubt.

"I tell you what, after you find out your out-date, make sure to get it to me," I told her. "I got a magic trick for you, and don't get all glassy-eyed either."

"Santiago." I heard my name being yelled out.

I walked to my cell door and looked out into the day room recreation area to see who was yelling my damn name like they got a problem.

I saw one of my favorite correctional officers standing in

the middle of the room with her hand on her hip.

"Santiago!" CO Jones yelled again. "Get your shit and get the fuck out my jail! You got five minutes, or I'll tell the people downstairs you don't want to go home today and to try again tomorrow!"

I always told Jones that if she was ever here when it was release time, to make it a grand spectacle, and she delivered.

"I don't even need five minutes, baby!" I responded in Boss Bitch fashion. "I'm ready to go as is. All my shit is at home already! It beat me there!"

"Let's go then, Santiago!" CO Jones hollered.

I looked at Jazmine and saw a mask on her face. I snatched her into a hug and held her tight.

"Bitch, you know everything I have is yours," I told her as I squeezed tighter. "You got my number, too, so swallow your pride and use it."

"I got you, bitch. Just don't be like the rest of these dream-smelling hoes that leave here. I'm gon' miss you!" Jazmine said, letting me go.

"Santiago!" CO Jones yelled. "I thought you ain't need five minutes?!"

"I can make time for this bitch right here!" I hollered. "Call me crazy, but she would be the only reason why I'm gon' miss this place!"

I used that as my last goodbye and began my strut across the floor and out of the door behind Jones.

"Bitch, you something else!" CO Jones said as the door closed behind us. "You really made an exit, didn't you?"

"These bitches don't like me, and I don't fuck with them,

so it's no love lost," I responded. "The bitch you seen me hug, though? That's my bitch! She been with me, and not against me since I stepped foot in this bitch."

"What's her name so I can take care of her for you?" she asked.

Jones was down like that. When a bitch needed something that was important, she was about helping those in need. So, I knew Jones was good people. Her telling me she would take care of Jazmine for me let me know moves were going to be made.

"Jazmine Wesley is her name," I told her. "I appreciate you offering to look after her. You still got my number?"

She just looked at me as we continued down the hall to the elevators.

We didn't say a word for the rest of the time she escorted me, and I understood fully. If people saw us just vibing like that, it would put her under the eye of those above her.

My mind switched. My lawyer said a few days, and there I was a 'few' hours later getting my discharge. That was one eviction I was glad to honor, and they didn't need to send no sheriff to escort me off the premises. If anything, they needed to throw me out the window and see if I could fly.

As the gate opened in front of me, I looked at Jones and winked. She remained blank-faced, but I could see the smile in her eyes.

At the window to get my belongings, the officer had me sign and thumbprint papers. When the bag came across the counter with my clothes and other things, I was all too happy to change that I almost stripped right there.

"You trying to get me fired!" the officer said. "Take your ass to the restroom! Crazy ass woman!"

I couldn't help but laugh but did as he said.

I felt close to being myself again after getting dressed in the outfit I was arrested in, a Prada pantsuit with matching shoes that were powder blue and my jewelry. I exited the restroom and returned the jail clothes to the officer with a smile.

"You missed a good show." I teased seductively.

"I bet I did, but I need my paycheck!" he replied with a laugh. "Now, get out of here before I change my mind and lose my job."

"I got one problem," I told the officer.

"What?" he asked seriously.

"I got arrested at home, so I don't have my phone or money to use." I began. "Is there a phone I could use to get a ride?"

He looked at me for a minute before responding, "I'm not supposed to do this. What's the number? I'll tell whoever it is that you got out and need a ride."

I gave him the number to my dad. As he dialed, I looked at the door to my freedom. So close, but so far away.

"Hey, he said you're in luck because he's right up the street." the officer informed me after a couple of minutes.

I damn near jumped the counter to kiss him full on the lips! Instead, I told him thank you and made my long-awaited exit to freedom.

The wait for my dad wasn't long. I didn't know where he was, and I didn't care, but it was like ten minutes before I saw his 600 Benz hit the corner. He wasn't at a complete stop before I jumped in.

"Don't even stop! I been here long enough!" I told him. "I want a long shower…"

I looked at my dad and saw something in his face I've seen since I was a kid.

My dad, or Papi as he was best known, at an even 6 feet with a muscular frame, was rarely stoned-faced with me. The quietness from him meant I needed to start over.

"I'm sorry, Papi. How you doing? You know I'm happy to see you and thankful you was able to pick me up. I'm just all too ready to get away from this nightmare." I let Papi know. "Where's Momma at?"

He remained quiet for a minute. When we caught the red light, he looked me in the eyes. His eyes were a startling green that gave him an intense look.

"Your mother and I are doing fine. What needs to be explained is why were you put into a position where you were charged with murder?!" His anger showed through his calm demeanor. "I hope you learned a lesson from your mistakes and wrong judgments."

That was it. My reprimand without a lecture. Papi had always been a man of few words, so when he spoke to you, listen intently for the hidden message in his words. What was said wasn't made for a response from me. Its intent was to have me think on what got me where I had just left and what would keep me from going back.

Papi was a cold-blooded gangster back in his day and still kept in contact with the streets even though he retired from it. All his money went into legit businesses, but he didn't live like he had money. When I asked why, he told me that there were already haters looking to take what little you had, so why show them your price tag and give them a bigger target to focus on? That was the best logic I've heard.

"Envy, I've accepted your lifestyle and choices. I've even endorsed the Madame role you hold now." Papi said, shocking me that he knew about my hustle. "Everyone is not built for the lives we live. That's why there are haters ready to hurt us. You were born into a hustler's family and raised in a hustler's household. That is why your mother and I gave you your lessons at a young age and attempted to hammer into your brain that if you chose this lifestyle, there was going to be people for you and others against you."

I listened full heartedly because I knew he was pulling my coat tail on what he found out while I was locked up.

"I told your mother I would talk to you and not be hard on you because you don't need tough love to learn." Papi continued. "Your mother wants blood for the betrayal you endured and ended up in jail for. Like I told her, that is your business, and you have to take care of it. Let me say this, and I'm done on the whole subject. Whatever you decide to do from this day about your situation, make sure your connections are solid and sound. Do you understand me?"

"Yes, Papi," I responded.

"Good, let's get you home. I told your mother you called me, and she insisted she cook you a meal 'cause she knows, like I do, how jail food tastes." Papi said with a smile.

Less than an hour later, we pulled up to my parent's

house. I had never been happier to see the hill the house sat on or the small woods that neighbor it. Seeing Momma's candy-apple red Lexus IS 250i sitting in the driveway under the carport brought a small smile across my face and eased the rest of my anxiety.

Nothing like the home you grew up in to ease all your worries and sadness.

I don't know if my mom, or Momma as I called her, was sitting by a window watching the street or something, 'cause as Papi pulled in his spot, Momma appeared as if by magic. In her hand was a dish towel, and on her beautiful dark brown face was a smile showing her pearly whites. Behind her, I could see the family dog, Queen. Queen was an all-white Pitbull that had been with us since my freshman year at high school. She was house-trained and didn't need a leash at all. Can you say properly trained and happy pet? Like Momma, Queen seemed happy to see Papi's car.

"One last thing before we get out of this car," Papi said. "Take care not to endanger yourself, believing you protecting me or your mother when you take care of your situation. We can take care of ourselves. Besides, whoever has the cajones to come our way will lose them in the worst possible way."

After parking, he didn't wait for a response and exited the car, leaving me sitting for a second too long. Momma's smile wavered, but Papi said something to her, and the smile was back in full bloom. She said something, and Queen was out the house and at the car door in half a second, tail wagging happily.

"Hey, my baby!" I greeted, opening the door and opening

my arms.

I was rewarded with licks that warmed my soul.

"I wish I could have got a greeting like that when you got in my car!" Papi said. When I looked up, I saw the smile on his face and laughter in his eyes. "All I received was a 'Papi, get me out of here!' command!"

"I love you too, Papi!" I responded, closing the car door. "Mommy love!"

"Don't mind your father none. You know his feelings for his only child!" Momma spoke with her thick accent, which came out when she was excited and happy. "He'd move the world if he could for you!"

I hugged Momma and got led inside.

"Go shower the jail off of you. The food will be ready in a little bit," Momma told me.

Of course, I obeyed without objection 'cause I needed a good cleansing. A good scrubbing with some real soap, shampoo, and conditioning.

"I'm home!"

CHAPTER TWO

After taking an hour-long bath, rubbing myself down with lotions and oils, and doing my hair, I made my way to the smell of food I knew so well. When I entered the living room, I got the surprise of my life.

"What the fuck are y'all doing here?!" I growled with attitude as a way of welcome.

There sat Tasha and Ivy, the two bitches who I knew set me up for the murder charge. I grew up with them, from diapers to bikers to riders. They were bitches I used to trust without a second thought of it.

"I invited them 'cause they are your friends, and watch your tongue in my house, Envy." Papi warned, glaring at me. The silent tone said it all.

"I apologize, Papi. As for these two snakes you let in the house, they need to get gone before it becomes a warzone!"

"You need to chill out! We ain't do a thang to you, contrary to belief!" This came from Ivy, our Left Eye look alike. Color, attitude, and all, including looks.

"That's real spit, Envy!" Tasha seconded. She was the tallest and thickest of us all with her dark brown complexion.

"Know what?!" I bit out, fed up with the foolishness altogether. "Y'all stay, I'll leave!"

I walked to the door to leave, only to hear a voice as strong as a hurricane and the same temperament.

"Envy Sinclaire!" Momma shouted. "You come here and explain yourself right now! You get out of jail, we invite your friends, and you act this way! Sit down!"

Momma didn't know the lifestyle I loved; she knew I hustled, but she never heard a peep. Regardless of what Papi thought he knew, he'd never understand the full scope of my grind. Before us three graduated, beating up other bitches and robberies put our name in the street. I was already in the shadow of my parents, so making a name for myself to show the hood I could hold my own was really detrimental to my health and life.

I knew Momma didn't get it, but I had to let her know why I felt some kind of way about them two in the house. I broke it down by giving Momma a quick summary of what I knew to have happened and why I was at odds with Tasha and Ivy.

During our last robbery, or at least one of our last robberies together, the nigga decided to play chicken and caught a bullet. Not being excited to gain our stripe in the public eye, we got creative on ways to get rid of the body. The river was out 'cause it still left evidence to wash ashore down the line. In the end, we went out to Cordoua in the middle of the woods with gasoline and burned the body.

Yeah, I pulled the trigger, but in Shelby County, accessory is just as bad as the crime itself. So, when the police came to my home and arrested me, I automatically thought they had me for human trafficking, not murder. So, imagine my reaction when they said murder, and they found the remains of the body. Exactly!

Given the breakdown, I saw Momma's expression change ever so slightly. Her eyes changed every minute as I detailed the source of my mistrust. Also, to see them still free, Momma knew I kept the code and kept my mouth closed.

Unlike these two bitches.

"Envy, now you know damn well we don't get down like that!" Ivy said, obviously desperate to be believed.

"What I know is that four people, plus God, know about the robbery and murder. Make that three, 'cause the fourth is dead and can't recount his own death!" I said sarcastically.

"So, you mean to tell me, dem gurls is the reason me baby was in tee jail for murder?" Momma asked us as her accent thickened, showing her anger for the first time. "Envy, I need chu sure dese gurls did wut you say dem did."

"Papi, with your contacts in the street, did you catch a whisper of this"? He shook his head no. "Momma, with the chicks you know, did you hear anything at all before now about something close to this?"

"No, Envy," she answered, looking at Tasha and Ivy.

"That don't mean we had something to do with it at all!" Tasha exclaimed.

"Ever since I upped my grind and elevated my hustle,

you bitches been jaded," I said as Momma left the room. "When I was with y'all, it was all good, but I'm not trying to crumb hustle my whole life."

"That's not fair, Envy!" Ivy spit out. "You left us hanging! Your day ones!"

The slip I was waiting for. A dumb motherfucker will always give their self up if you get them mad enough.

"My true day ones would have been happy I was doing better and would have tried to up their grind right along with me. Not try and ruin my life going to the police and getting me arrested for murder!" I shot back as Momma came back into the room with her hand slightly behind her back.

Papi saw what I saw and went to her and whispered some words to her. She shook her head in response, and I knew that if these bitches didn't leave, it was going to be a double homicide in the house the day I got out of jail. Not a good look. As I was getting my next words ready, I made it a point to go to the door and open it.

"You two need to get out and don't come here no more or anywhere near me," I warned them.

"You always thought you was better than us," Ivy said, passing me and going out the door. "You seen us as your lame partnas instead of your friends."

"No, I always knew I was better than the hustle we got comfortable with, and I proved it," I responded. "So, if that makes me better than y'all, then so be it."

"Bitch, you forgot where you came from!" Tasha said directly in my face.

It took all my control not to mop the floor with the bitch's face. See, that statement was dumb on her part because hustle was still in the hood, and here I was at my parent's house in the hood.

"Let me say this, and I'm done with this and y'all." I stepped out the door, ready for a reaction. "You bitches are crumb hustlers comfortable eating crumbs, and I wasn't. I like a full meal, and I wanted a buffet, so I worked my brain for something bigger. Instead of you hoes riding with me, you chose to remain on the crumbs. I upgraded, and y'all stagnated. In case your simple minds don't comprehend, I leveled up, and y'all still stuck counting pennies. Now, goodbye and good riddance. Snakes ain't welcomed here."

"Bitch!" Tasha made her move.

Instinct took over, but before any punches were thrown, the unmistakable sound of a gun cocking stopped us dead.

"It'll be best if you girls leave before my wife loses her patience and have your family planning your funerals if they find the bodies." Papi spoke from behind Momma, who had a gun with a nice hole at the end of it, pointed at the bitches as Papi spoke. And to emphasize the threat, Momma tilted her head sideways as if questioning how they wanted this to end.

Turning around, I spoke as calmly as I felt, telling them, "Get in your car and leave. Oh, but believe this, if nothing else. You will get what you got coming to you."

They kept quiet, got in their car, and quickly left, knowing that one word would end it here in the driveway. Smart bitches.

****

After letting my parents know the full scope of what was going on, I could see the different way that they saw me.

Hell, I would too if my only child told me about how they started hustling, selling weed, and robbing, and now they were a Madame with men and women in their employ. All the while getting ready to expand again once I gain a good dope connect. I been in the game for 10 years, since middle school, and I worked my was up on my new hustle within the last year. Riding with Tasha and Ivy, I made a name for myself outside of being my parent's little girl.

Though Papi said he knew my lifestyle, I could tell he didn't know completely 'cause I didn't put my business out there. I been grinding since I was 14, but he thought I started hustling a couple of years out of high school. Momma, on the other hand, was clueless to my hustle. Reason being, because she was completely out of the streets but still had it in her.

"Papi," I said after explaining my situation to my parents. "I need to use the phone so I can make a phone call or two."

Without a word, Papi handed me his phone, grabbed Momma by the hand, and went into the kitchen.

My first call was to my lawyer, and the next would be to one of my workers I left in charge of the business.

"Timberly Davis, Attorney at Law. How may I help you?" my attorney answered after a couple of rings.

"Ms. Davis, this me, Ms. Santiago," I responded. "I don't know what you did, but I was released about an hour or so ago."

"I just did my job." she began. "The evidence they had was zero to none. All they had was the words of Ms. Jones and Ms. Clark saying you did it, which was not enough to have charged you without a full investigation.

I remained silent, letting that soak in. So, I could be charged later on down the line if they found evidence that I was involved.

Not a good look.

"Now what happens from here is that they can, and will, keep you as a primary suspect because your name was put in to say you did it by supposed eyewitnesses," She continued. "I'll keep my eye on it, and if you need anything, call me."

"Thank you," I responded. "I do need some information, but it's not about my case."

"If I can help, I will," she answered.

"Jazmine Wesley," I started. "If there is anything I can do to help, would you let me know? As far as payments for you or whatever is needed to get her out of the jam she's in."

"That would have to be her choice. She's already paid me for her case, and I'm doing all I can," she said. "So, you have to talk to her."

"I will, but I want you to let her know that I've talked to you, and whatever y'all need in terms of help, I'm available," I told her.

"I'll do that. Was there anything else?" my lawyer asked.

"No, that's all for now. Thank you," I answered.

"Okay, well, you be careful and be in touch," she said.

"Thanks, bye," I responded, ending the call.

My next call was to my phone to check my messages. When I got through, I had five messages worth returning, but I'd handle that when I got home and my phone. The last call was to my place of business.

Platinum Services. We catered to almost all things entertainment-wise. The escort service was a by-product called Diamond Escorts. Located in the shopping complex up the street from my home, which was the main office.

Three rings in, the phone was answered by my second in command, also known as the business manager.

"Platinum Services. This is Kyle speaking. How may I help you?" He answered in his trademark baritone voice, which could make most women cream from the sound of it.

"Nigga, cut the sweet shit, it's me," I said playfully, letting him know he could relax. "I'm glad you learned some manners, though."

You could hear the laughter deep in his chest over the line before he responded.

"Damn, boss. It's good to hear your voice," He began. "When did you get out?"

"A few hours ago, give or take," I answered. "I need everybody to meet at the Diamond House tonight around seven."

"That can happen. We ain't got any appointments lined up for tonight anyway, so I'll make the calls," Kyle answered. "Anything else?"

"Not off the top of my head, but stay close to your phone," I responded. "I'll call back in a few." Not waiting for a response, as usual, I ended the call. I hoped all business was good. I made Kyle manager when he showed me he was on his shit top-notch.

****

Kyle had just got out of prison in Texas before he made his way up here. He actually tried to rob me at a red light out in Orange Mound on my way back from dropping some of my girls off. Little did he know that when he jumped in the passenger seat, my pistol was in my lap. By the time he sat down, it was touching the side of his head. When he spoke, trying to make his bound, I heard his accent in his bass tone. He explained that he had only been in Tennessee a few days, as I had my Chrome .380 pointed at him. I shocked him when I asked if he wanted a job. When the light turned green, I began to drive.

"Close the door," I told him. "What's your name since you in my car?"

"Kyle, but people who know me call me King Kai," he answered.

"Against my better judgment, I'm gon' put my pistol back in my lap and ask you again," I said, paying attention to the road. "Do you want a job?"

"Doing what?" he answered.

"For one, you ain't gon' be risking your life unless absolutely necessary," I answered. "I run an escort service, men and women, and hire out to the strip clubs around the city. Seeing as you like to play with pistols and be a street nigga, you'll fit in nicely with the boys I got and can play a little security on the side."

"I ain't no hoe, shorty, feel me…." he began before I cut him off.

"Neither are the niggas that work for me. They like fucking chicks and getting paid, though," I cut in. "I'm a Boss Bitch that fuck with Boss Niggas, my guy. If you can't see the big picture instead of being narrow-minded, I can pull over and let you out."

****

A year later, Kyle made his way up to being my business manager, overseeing the escorts and security I provided to different clientele. When I got put on lock, he made sure my books were lined and all the business was taken care of. The only thing I hadn't let him touch yet was the drug game.

If it wasn't for him, I would have opened my own strip club in the hood. So, instead of sharing money with other clubs, the money stayed in-house. We wanted to attract the money of a certain caliber, so I named it Diamond House. A two-story strip club where downstairs, the women danced, and upstairs, the men danced.

"Envy," Papi said, snapping me out of my thoughts. "Are you staying the night, or do I need to take you home?"

Looking at his phone, I saw the time was 2:20 pm.

"I'll need you to take me home, Papi, but not yet," I answered. "Another hour or so."

"Okay," he responded, leaving the room again.

Knock! Knock! Knock!

"I got it!" I said, getting up from the sofa at the same time that Queen bolted into the room and passed me to the door.

Not bothering to ask who it was, I opened the door, knowing at the first sign of bullshit, Queen was gon' attack without a signal. But when I saw who it was, I was more surprised than anything. I guess the look showed on my face cause the smile that crossed their face was the response I received.

Derek, known as D-Wild around the hood and city. Also, my parents' neighbor's son. I hadn't seen him since he joined the Marines.

Boy, did he grow up and out!

"What's up, Envy? I ain't expect you to open the door." He said, still smiling.

He stood an even six feet and was muscular. Tyson Beckford fine! His hair was cut in a low Caesar fade with waves going 360 that would make a fish seasick. He wore a muscle shirt, basketball shorts, and some red and gray Jordans. He had a neatly trimmed and groomed goatee that kept him looking young but gave him a mature look at the same time.

"Long time no see, D-Wild," I responded with my own smile. "How long you been back from the Marines, soldier boy?"

"Long enough to get me a spot around the corner and hear about Envy putting in work." He answered. "And catch all the bullshit you been through."

"Let's go down the driveway," I told him, motioning for Queen to enter the yard. Closing the door and watching Queen take off into the yard, nose down, tail up, I became curious. "What brings you over here?"

"I asked your pops to hit me up when you came through so I could fuck with you," He answered. "I hope it ain't a problem."

"Nah, it's cool," I answered, turning to face him. "What's really good with you then?"

"I had two reasons to catch up with," He said with a smile. "Really, three."

When I cocked my eyebrows, he continued.

"One, I wanted to check on you personally. Two, I wanted to let you know if you need some help in any shape, size, form, or fashion, I got you." He said, looking off down the driveway. "Third, I wanted to talk business with you."

By D-Wild being older than me by five years, I got to see firsthand how he put in work before he finally left for the Marines. His name spoke for itself, D-Wild. The nigga had a reputation as strong as, if not stronger than, King Kong bred with Godzilla. His hustle was second to none. His fight game was ice water, and when it came to gunplay, you would rather face a gun squad blindfolded. By him being in the Marines, I just knew he had developed into a bigger monster.

"How bout this," I started. "Give me a ride to my house, and we can see what comes out of our meeting."

I looked in his parents' driveway and saw the black-on-black Custom 2006 Dodge Magnum, rims decked out. So, I already knew his paper was good, but to do business, I needed to see what he was on and about now.

"That's a bet." He responded. "When you gon' be ready?"

"As soon as I put Queen in and say bye to Papi and Momma," I answered. "I'll be back."

One quick whistle and Queen dashed across the yard and was by my side. When I headed to the door, she followed.

When I got in the house, my parents were in their usual seats. Papi looked at me blank-faced, and Momma gave me one of those looks like she wanted to play matchmaker.

"Derek gon' take you home?" Papi asked.

"Yes, Papi," I answered, walking to him to give him his phone. "And momma, you can stop looking at me like I'm gon' make him your son-in-law."

"Me neva said a word," she said, smiling. "You did."

"Anyway," mockingly rolling my eyes, I let them know, "I'm going to go ahead and leave."

I walked to both of them in turn and gave them hugs and kisses.

"I'll call when I get home," I said, heading back to the door.

"Don't bother, baby girl," Papi told me. "Just remember our talk and call if you need anything."

"Alright," I responded as I exited the house.

When I stepped outside, I noticed that D-Wild had parked in my parents' driveway and had the motor running. I could also hear the slight hum of his music coming from the car.

Approaching the car, he popped the locks. When I opened the door, a cloud of smoke came flowing out. The sweet smell of Memphis' finest herb assaulted my nostrils and led me in like Toucan Sam to his Fruit Loops. He was listening to T.I.'s "About the Money". He never turned the music down but looked at me like, 'What's up?' so I got it and closed the door. As I was closing the door, he passed me the blunt he was smoking and reversed down the driveway.

Waiting 'til the song was over, we just smoked and passed the blunt back and forth. When the song ended, he asked where we were headed. When I told him where I lived, he looked shocked and told me he lived on the same street a couple of houses down.

CHAPTER THREE

As D-Wild pulled behind my candy blue Audi, he gave a low whistle. "That's a nice whip," he said.

"Thanks," I responded. "That ain't shit. Wait 'til you see what I got in the garage."

When he turned off the car, his radio face disappeared into the dash. He pushed a button, and a stash spot opened, revealing half an ounce of herb and two packs of cigarillos. He grabbed those as I exited the car, waiting to get into my house to change clothes. After locking his car, he caught up with me at the front door as I was opening it.

"Close and lock the door for me," I told him as I walked in. "Make yourself at home while I go change. I'll be back so we can talk."

"Cool," he answered.

When I entered my room, I closed the door and stripped naked so I could change out of everything I went to jail in. Not wanting to dress professional, I opted for casual, comfortable, which meant True Religion jeans, with a tank top and True Religion jean jacket to match and ice white air forces to match the tank top.

Hood, but still classy.

Everything else I needed was in the kitchen, where I had been before I got arrested, everything except for my .380. I went into my closet, opened my safe, and grabbed my pistol and an extra clip.

After checking myself, I walked out of the room and found D-Wild sitting on the sofa with herb in front of him, rolling blunts. He had four rolled when I walked in and was working on a fifth when he looked and seen me.

"You clean up nice," he said. "Who the pistol for?"

"Not you, so you don't have to even worry about it," I answered as I continued to the kitchen to grab my purse. "You want something to drink?"

"You got hen?" he asked.

"I got you," I responded.

After pouring us both drinks, I grabbed my purse and headed back to the living room.

"So," I said by way of starting a conversation as I handed him his drink. "You wanted to talk business with me." I continued as I sat down. "The only reason I'm entertaining this is because I've known you since I was in diapers. So, what's the business?"

D-Wild finished the blunt he was rolling, making it a total of six in front of him. He sparked the freshly rolled and got up. When he handed it to me, I accepted it, and he went back to his seat, grabbed another, and sparked up before he spoke.

"Ya know, I have my own money," he said. "I'm looking to invest it somewhere. Even when I left, I kept my ears to the street about the city. I kept an eye on who was doing what." He continued as I hit my blunt. "Long story short, word is that you looking for a live connect, and I may be able to help with that."

"How do you propose to do that?" I asked, taking another hit of the blunt he gave me. "Unless you can get your hands on some real weight, and I ain't talking a few days, you can't help me."

"That's where my investment comes in," he said with a smile. "Give me a number. It ain't gotta be the exact number, but shoot something out there."

"20 bricks at 16.5 a piece," I said, pulling on the blunt, which was some damn good.

"330 grand for full grip, but my investment will have you paying 220 grand," he said, hitting his blunt and then taking a sip of his hen.

"Nice numbers," I replied. "40 pounds at eight a piece?"

"32,000, but you ain't payin' but 20," he answered confidently.

The numbers I wanted were smaller than that, but I wanted to see what kind of investment he was talking. He basically had it where I would pay 11 grand a brick and 500 a pound, which was love in this city. Those were damn near the same numbers this nigga out of Texas was shooting, only cheaper on the pounds and more on the bricks. If I took D-Wild's offer, it would be on the bricks, and I'd fuck with the

Texas nigga on the pounds.

"How do you plan to invest?" I asked. "As a silent partner. If so, I don't work for nobody else's money but my own. If you invest, you gon' be putting work in, soldier boy."

"Envy," he said, finishing his drink. "You ain't kept your ears to the street."

My look must have said enough.

"Check this out," he continued as he put his blunt out. "I know you run a company called Platinum Services with Diamond Escorts and Diamond House under the company logo. You got a hair spot called The Red Carpet that caters to men and women. Honestly, I didn't know where you live, but I do know you keep five rooms in the hotel on Airway for your girls and niggas to work out of and take clientele."

Dumbfounded, I was at a loss for words, but I didn't let it show. So, in true Boss Bitch fashion, I followed his lead and put my blunt out before I spoke.

"Okay, you did your homework on my places of business, but if your ears were really to the street, you would know the extent of my business and financial capabilities," I said, locking eyes with D-Wild. "You missed that I have trap houses ready for work around the hood and in Da Haven as well. See, the things that you heard on the street are things I let be known."

D-Wild just sat there with a smile on his face that always melted me when I was younger. It still did, but it seemed he wasn't finished.

"700 grand plus," he said with a satisfied look.

"What?" I asked, confused.

"That's your net worth." He told. "All businesses included in the count I last got."

This nigga had to be really connecting deep with somebody in order to get information like that. From waiting to gain a connect, I had an empty hole with no money flowing into it.

"As I said, I keep my ears to the street. The streets talk to me loud and clear." He said, reaching for another blunt. He sparked up and took a deep pull of the herb. "You don't know, but I used to run for your pops. He gave me the game, so when he left the game, I took the reigns and kept it going."

I didn't know how to feel about that, but as a Boss, I knew where he was headed and how to think.

"Pass me one of those and finish explaining," I told him.

"Me going to the Marines accomplished two things," D-Wild spoke, passing me the sparked blunt he lit. Grabbing another, he continued, "That made my money legit. It let me invest in different money and collect sums without suspicion. I'm a man about cash."

Unnerved, I looked him in the eye and knew I fell in love right there.

"I like that slick shit you talking, but let me explain something to you." I began, knowing that my next words had to be something Boss Bitch standard. He put me in full drive. "I'm a Boss Bitch; business over stupid shit. You still never answered the question I asked. How do you plan to invest in my business and put in work? Cause I don't work for nobody, my guy."

"Baby, I'm the plug," D-Wild said, taking a pull of the

blunt as he leaned forward to make sure he had eye contact. "All the money I sent back is drug money. In the last five years, I put in my game. 500,000 easy. That's just the money I put in, not got back." Without breaking eye contact, he stood up and walked over to me. He sat down right next to me. "I'm investing me."

He didn't even let me respond because I could see he was feeling himself, and I was feeling him, too. He left my senior year at high school for the Marines before I could reach the age to come to him.

"I've always wanted to tell you this, but I was away, and I thought it better if I came home in person and approached you correctly." He continued, "I know you a Boss 'cause you ain't have a choice in being one since your family is made of them. As a Boss Bitch, you look for like-minded souls that can vibe on the same wavelength without static. I am that like-minded soul for you."

"D-Wild, you know Papi would not like you fucking with me or how you talking," I reminded him. "I admit, I been on you for years, but you left."

"Your pops gave me his blessing a year ago when I told him I want to date you," he responded. "He respected I came on some old school respect, approaching him for your hand."

Little did D-Wild know that was how you got a date or wife in the Dominican Republic. Without the father's blessing, it would look like you poisoned the daughter's mind.

"I want to be the King to your Queen. I'm a Boss nigga, born and bred. Ya know my resume," He continued, leaning towards me and causing my temperature to rise. "I see it in your eyes that your mind is made up, so don't deny the feeling."

That made me snap alive.

"Not to be rude or kill the mood," I said, standing up. I had to compose myself before I made that dive. I knew I wouldn't come up for air. "Go home and get dressed, and come back over here. We're going to the Diamond House. Dress as you feel."

"Really?" he questioned with a smile.

"Really," I responded. "You ain't think it was going to be that easy, did you?" I raised the statement with a laugh.

"I was hoping you wouldn't make it easy for me," he said, standing. "I've been waiting too long to show you how I move, sweetheart."

When he finally left, I had to take a deep breath and get myself back on track. I couldn't afford to be caught slipping yet.

****

After showering and dressing in an egg-white Prada pantsuit with matching six-inch heels, my phone rang as I reached for my jewelry. D-Wild's name and picture came up on my screen as Kelly Rowland's "Motivation," the ringtone I set for him, played.

"Yeah," I answered, putting him on speakerphone.

"I'm bout to step out my door right now heading your way," D-Wild responded. "Are you decent, or will I catch you in your robe?"

Before I could answer, he continued with a laugh.

"Don't answer that. I'll see for myself," he said.

I couldn't help but smile because the thoughts I had of D-Wild when I was coming up were nothing short of him walking in on me in my birthday suit.

"I know you would like that, and maybe even dreamed of that, but…" I said as I grabbed my Cartier bracelet to put on. "I don't think you need that kind of distraction."

In response, he gave a deep laugh that had me biting my lip.

"The distraction would only be the robe," he remarked. "And after that's gone, I'll be able to fully concentrate on you. In every way possible."

"Bye, boy!" I said, not letting him rattle me too much. "Ring the bell when you get to the door."

By way of answer, my doorbell rang.

"How long have you been standing there?" I asked with a smile.

"Since you answered your phone," he answered. "Just wanted to give you a little more time to get ready if you needed it."

"Such the gentleman," I commented, smirking. "Here I come."

After I had ended the call and put in my last earring, a thought passed through my head. I grabbed the Chanel No. 5 and sprayed a modest amount. Just enough to grab attention, but not a lot to where it caused a headache.

I'm a Boss Bitch, not an attention whore.

With one last look into the mirror for inspection, I headed to the front door to let D-Wild in. Not wanting to have to stay longer in the house, I grabbed my pocketbook and keys from the kitchen counter on the way to the door. Opening the door, I had to do a double take.

D-Wild had on a three-piece, tailor-made, custom Italian-cut Giorgio Armani smoke gray suit that wrapped around his six-foot muscular frame. On his feet were a pair of Mauri grey snake skins that didn't take away from the suit but surprisingly gave it the kick it needed. He had a simple white gold necklace and the appropriate size earrings in his ears. On his wrists were a white gold Rolex and a white gold bracelet with baguets. It made you notice the diamond cufflinks that finished his look of GQ professionalism. Just looking at him made me want to say fuck going to the Diamond House and snatch his ass to let him make love to me like his body language said it could.

I must have stood there too long because the smile that made his eyes shine told me I gave him the response he was looking for. So, in 'Boss Bitch' fashion, I made my regroup.

"You clean up nice, D-Wild." I complimented him. "Who knew you had it in you?"

"Thank you. You clean up beautifully yourself," D-Wild responded smoothly. "And you can call me Derek when we're by ourselves or in a business meeting. I'm only D-Wild on two occasions."

"Yeah, and when are those?" I asked.

"In the streets and in the bedroom," he said seductively with a twinkle in his eyes. "Hopefully, in the future, you can enjoy the latter."

Ladies and gentlemen of the jury. I'm a Boss Bitch, born

and bred. I've never been a sucker fish a day in my life. This brother brought something so hot out of me that if you put me in an ice bath, I could turn it into a jacuzzi.

"Okay, Derek, slow down for me," I remarked, motioning him to come in and follow me. "I see you had a lot of practice with your game, and it's pretty good," I continued as I led him to the garage. "If I didn't have my focus, I'll be honest with you. I'd fuck your brains out."

Opening the door leading to the garage, I stopped as if considering what I just said.

"As I said before, you don't need the distraction." I continued through the door into the garage, where my baby was waiting. "I'm not your average woman. Business before pleasure, baby boy."

Pressing the garage door opener on the wall, the light came on, showing my cocaine white-on-white 745 BMW with the mirror-tinted windows. Everything on and in my car was custom-made for me personally. My break pads had my name on them, and my plates said the same. My trunk was cocaine white with six twelve-inch Boss speakers in a custom box powered by three 200v Boss amps. The leather inside was cocaine white with matching carpet, and to keep it hood classic, I put in wood grain on the steering wheel, across the dash, and on all four doors.

Before I could finish admiring my baby, Rick Ross's "Hustlin" ringtone came from my phone. Pulling it out and looking at the screen, Kyle's face showed.

"Get in," I instructed D-Wild before answering my phone. "Hello?"

"We all here. Is there anything specific you need before you get here?" Kyle asked as I got in and push started my car.

"Yeah, I'm bringing company, and he likes his Hennessey," I answered. "For me, the usual."

"Got you. See you soon." Kyle replied, ending the call.

Before I reversed out of the garage, I had to get my ride-out music on first. So, I did a CD change, and Rich Homie's "Can't Judge Her" came through the speakers. For all who don't know, this song was for the Boss Bitches that remember where they come from and hustle hard to get that paper--regardless of what the hustle is. That was why I made it my ride-out song in the first place.

Don't judge me.

Pulling out of the garage and down the driveway, D-Wild just sat back and motioned the question of if he could smoke. Getting the go-ahead, he pulled a box out of his suit's inside pocket, removed a blunt to smoke, and handed it to me. After I accepted it, he pulled another for himself.

After we had both sparked and settled in for the ride, there were no words that needed to be said.

CHAPTER FOUR

Pulling into the Diamond House parking lot with the bass line of Wale's "Bag of Money" announcing my presence, I had already decided to take D-Wild on his offer for two reasons.

First, the profit margin he gave me was adequate and substantial.

Second, I wanted the brother in my bed and in me.

Parked in the parking space reserved for me, I turned my music down to be rewarded with a smile from D-Wild.

"What?" I asked, turning off the car.

"Every song you played is about a woman with her own, not needing a nigga unless absolutely needed," He responded. "Is that you telling me who you are and what you need or don't need?"

This was the part every Boss Bitch put in my position would love. The moment where you have a man all ears, at full attention, listening and following every word that you say.

Always make it count 'cause you only get one shot at it to do it right.

Especially when you knew it was a test of wits and intellect.

So, knowing that the stage was set for me to show D-Wild that I was not the girl he remembered from years ago but a full-grown woman and Boss, I looked him directly into his eyes before I educated him.

"Derek, I want you to pay close attention to what I'm about to say and enlighten you on," I began, getting comfortable in my seat. "I know I told you I am a Boss Bitch, but let me explain it to you. The songs you were listening to don't even come close to who I am or the mentality I have set for myself. I'm independent. I've bought everything I have, nothing rented. The way I see it, I don't need a man to upgrade so I can do bigger and better things. A man needs a woman like me so he can be complete and elevate his game."

I paused to make sure D-Wild was still at attention. To my surprise, he hadn't stopped smiling since I started.

"Chicks always say they bossin', or bad, or whatever, but they always look for a man to save them like they Cinderella or some shit," I said, on a roll. "So, when you hear Webbie and Lil' Boosie talking bout bad bitches, they speaking on my lifestyle, but not on me. Money is my motivation and has always been my topic for discussion. That's the true meaning of Business before Pleasure. Bitches got it backward, trying to trap a nigga with the pussy and looking for a handout. If a man can't respect my mind and my hustle, knowing that he's around one of a dying breed, then I don't need him, and he can go to find one of the starstruck ass bitches to play with."

During my whole presentation, not one time did D-Wild lose eye contact or his smile.

"Long story short, I'm a Boss Bitch for real. Born and Bred," I stated with a smile of my own. "When it come to the game, I don't just say this shit, I play this shit."

"You know," D-Wild started when he was sure I had finished my say. "I want to put in my application if you're accepting any."

"Boy..." I started before being cut off.

"No, hear me out. I listened to you with respect, so I should receive the same honor," he said and continued when I motioned that he had the floor. "I'm letting you know I want to put my application in to be your man. I'm glad you have the mentality to not make it easy for me, and that's what I respect about you. We don't have to have a discussion about this now 'cause, as you said, it's Business before Pleasure, and we still have business to discuss. So, let's take care of that so we can get to the topic about us."

That said, D-Wild opened his door and got out of the car in true Boss fashion, leaving me thinking I finally found a King deserving of a Queen of my caliber and breed.

I couldn't let him believe he had me shaken in any size, shape, form, or fashion when I stepped out the car. So, instead of rushing, I moved with practiced ease, showing that I still had control. As he followed me to the club entrance, I gave an extra sway of my hips 'cause he earned it.

Before we got to the door, they were opened by Kyle. He took one look at D-Wild and looked at me with a cocked eyebrow. Questioning, customer, client, or other.

"Where is everybody?" I said as an answer to his unasked question.

"In the back..." Kye responded, then motioned to the stage. "Dorian, Michael, and Calvin are over there shooting dice though. They the only ones up front."

"Get everybody to the front then," I instructed, making my way to the dice game that was in full swing.

They never noticed my approach, and I didn't interrupt them as I sat down in front of the stage. D-Wild took a seat next to me and smiled while watching the game.

"Point 10, nigga!" Michael announced, shaking the dice. "I bet Big Ben and Lil Joe, but back door ain't cheating!"

"I put a Ben on that both ways!" Dorian responded as the fader. "You want some Calvin?"

"Fuck it!" he said after a second. "I bet he hit Big Ben for a Frank."

"You betta ride wit me, my guy!" Michael said, letting the dice roll.

After the first roll misses point, Dorian screamed, "Y'all both just lost this bread, Fred!"

"Bet another Ben if you sho!" Michael retorted, shaking the dice.

"Bet!" Dorian accepted.

"Point 10, and I win, Lil Joe get more!" Michael said, rolling the dice.

When the dice stopped, Dorian just put his head down.

"Pick your money up, Cal, my guy!" Michael said, grabbing money off the floor and leaving one. "Bet back,

Dee?"

"Nah, y'all done for now," I responded, bringing my presence to their attention. "We got a meeting to take care of."

In unison, all eyes snapped in my direction.

The first to break the silence was Calvin.

"Fucking right!" Calvin jumped up, shouting. "Damn, we missed you, boss! Now, tell us who we got to ride on for this shit."

At 5'9", with dark brown skin and 190 on his frame, Calvin was the quietest but the quickest to ride out and put in work. Michael was his cousin. At 6'2", 220, built like a football player with the same dark brown skin, you would mistake them for brothers. Dorian was the wild card of the click. At an even 6' with light brown skin and a boxer's build, he was the first to pull his heat at all times.

I met all three one day outside a strip club I was trying to get this chick from to work for me. While waiting for the chick to come out, I decided to take a little walk to pass the time. When I hit the corner, I walked into them, beating the shit out of another nigga while the girl I was trying to get at was standing back watching. Upon seeing me, chick ran up and told me that the dude getting his ass beat was trying to force her to fuck with him. Dorian, Michael, and Calvin happened to walk up and commenced to beating that ass. When they was done, they checked his pockets, took all his money, and gave it to the chick. They kept his license, telling him that if the shit was reported, they would pay him a visit. Shit, seeing that, I made them an offer I hoped they wouldn't refuse.

Which brought us to now.

"Hell yeah!" Dorian said with a smile. "Whoever the reason that the doll was put in chains needs to be put on ice ASAP!"

Michael never said a word. He came right to me, bent down, and hugged me. When he let go, he looked me in the eyes.

Another thing about Michael was he stayed connected to the streets so well that he might have gotten the full 411 on my situation, and looking in his eyes, I believed he did. He just hadn't told the rest. He left that for me.

Kyle, being my saving grace, announced his incoming, not knowing he saved two lives or just extended them from being taken so soon.

Behind him were three bitches whose reputations came to me through Kyle himself. They were some chicks he called up from Texas that he said was down by law. They proved their work, but I knew that their initial loyalty lay with Kyle first... It worried me initially, but then it didn't because I had all the backup I needed with Dorian, Michael, and Calvin.

"Here we go, boss," Kyle said, making his way to us. "Everybody here and ready for the meeting."

Vanessa was the first to notice D-Wild sitting next to me.

"Who do we have here?" Vanessa asked, acknowledging D-Wild with a seductive undertone. "Never seen him before."

Vanessa was a professional at seduction. With a body straight out of a "show" magazine, caramel coloring on a 5'7" frame, and a face of natural beauty, she was what I called "A nigga's worst setup."

When she made her comment, it brought Kayla and Jordan to attention.

"Damn, he fine," Jordan said, bringing up the rear while Kayla remained quiet. "Boss lady, is that you, or is he open for engagement?"

Jordan was a skin beauty standing 5'5' with a thick frame that had enough jiggle but enough shape not to be called a fat girl.

"Girl, I saw him first," Vanessa said, never taking her eyes off D-Wild once.

"May I?" D-Wild asked me.

"Be my guest," I answered, wanting to see what he had.

He chose to remain seated as he addressed the girls, but a smile didn't touch his face.

"My name is Derek, but everybody that knows me calls me D-Wild." He began. I could tell the name meant something to Dorian, Michael, and Calvin because they came to attention and gave me a look.

"I just look like this if you seeing a victim. I'm nowhere near it," he continued. "To answer the question of being open for engagement, I am, but not for any of y'all. Don't take that wrong cause y'all holding something, but what I'm looking for is in my sights already. So, can we move on?"

"Envy, I don't know who bro is, but I like him," Kayla finally spoke up. "Homey must be built Ford tough the way he talking."

Kayla was a redbone with a body like Halle Berry, standing at 5'9". Her skin was flawless. She had a couple leg tattoos that were tasteful, one on her lower back that said "Money Goes Here" and an arrow pointing down in a tribal fashion.

"Derek been my neighbor my whole life until he went to the Marines five years ago," I explained to the room, getting on with the meeting. "Now, he's back, and we're neighbors again. He came to me with a business proposition, but first, I want to make sure that everything has still been on point."

"Nothing slowed down after you left," Kyle responded. "In fact, we already made quota and looking to go over."

"Dorian?" I asked.

"We ready to open Platinum Services Security whenever you ready," he answered. "We actually did a trial run and loaned ourselves out separately to a couple parties to put the name out there."

"What about the spots I asked you to fill?" I asked, referring to him putting people in the trap spots.

"That was done while you was on lock," Calvin answered. "Just waiting on work to give out."

Letting the information be filed, I noticed Michael looking at Kyle as he folded his arms.

"Okay. Spit it out," I remarked. "Whatever it is."

I get silence in return.

"Michael?" I asked.

"Had to disappear some niggas after they came here trying to snatch up a few girls," Michael stated dispassionately. "Said them chicks was choosing 'cause the locked eyes and was entertaining conversations."

"Before you go ballistic," Dorian interjected, "We ain't

disappear 'em because they was pimps. When we told 'em the girls was spoken for, one of 'em pulled out a knife and went at Calvin 'cause he was closest."

I could imagine how that went. Even though Calvin was the smallest, I've seen him take care of a few big problems at the club without any help.

Pimps been a constant problem for me ever since they found out a woman owned the Diamond House. When the first pimp found out, he told me I should choose up and be his bottom bitch and show the rest of his hoes how to make his money. After I gave him an extensive Boss Bitch lecture that he would never forget, I had Kyle escort him to his car and off the premises. So, a pimp trying to poach one of my girls wasn't a surprise. Hell, I've poached a few girls from other clubs. To disappear one, though...

"Just tell me it didn't get done here," I said, hopeful.

Everyone, including Calvin, looked at me like I should have known better than to ask that question or make that comment.

Enough said. Or not said, for that matter.

"Okay, down to business," I stated to the room. "Derek, you got the floor. What was your proposition?"

****

Watching D-Wild control the room showed me that Papi taught him well, and he was on his best shit. Nobody interrupted him as he told his intentions and what he was willing to provide. As he talked business, my mind was already at a decision on both business and pleasure. Ground rules would need to be set to come together and build an empire, but I felt it could be done 'cause we were on the same page.

Ladies and gentlemen of the jury, don't judge me just yet. Leave your verdicts open as we continue down this road of absolute potential, which this situation has a lot of.

After that decision was made, the problem of Ivy and Tasha rose to the forefront of the list of things that needed to be taken care of behind my murder charge. True enough, the charges got dismissed, but the code and consequences for betrayal were simple. The streets don't like snitches at all. They are what's wrong with the game. For every big money downfall, there has been a snitch in the background, turning state evidence.

Not so much as hearing, but sensing D-Wild bring his presentation to a close a good thirty minutes later, I snapped out of my thoughts to catch the last of his words.

"If my numbers don't fit into what y'all trying to do, I'll take suggestions as well as negotiate more." D-Wild was saying. "But I doubt it necessary 'cause while my numbers are low and showing love, they are high on the profit margin. Any questions?"

At first, there was a collective silence around the room. This was what I wanted to see, the reaction to his proposal to others.

"I'm liking those numbers, my guy," Dorian spoke, being the first to break the silence. "My only question is why Envy ain't already take you up on your offer?"

"Well, when I came at her with it, she told me to roll with her here," D-Wild explained. "So, I assumed she was bringing me to meet her business partners to discuss it with."

I could see the wheels turning in Dorian's head, and this was how I always knew he was the leader of his group. All three were smart as a whip and had more snap than a spoken word seminar, but Dorian was more confident with his thoughts and words.

"Okay, I can see her reasoning," Dorian finally said. "By being dope boys, we can see the full picture of what you're working with and know what kind of profit came with it," he paused, considering a thought before continuing. "I don't understand what roles she wants Kyle, Vanessa, Kayla, and Jordan to play, but I figure they figuring that out for themselves."

I remained silent, allowing myself to observe if everybody would understand their roles or if I would have to point them in the right direction. Dorian didn't disappoint. Now, it was up to Kyle to snap to attention and catch his role along with the girls he brought in.

D-Wild looked at me, and I gave my attention to Kyle, who was sitting on the stage with his arms folded and face frowned up in concentration. You could tell when he came to his conclusion because he smiled to himself and chuckled before he started to speak.

Make me proud, King Kai.

"Stop me if I'm off track even by a centimeter, Envy," Kyle started off first. "We gon' be washing the money through all the companies under Platinum Services, for one, and that's my role. Vanessa, Kayla, and Jordan are to move some product through the Diamond House, Diamond Escorts, and The Red Carpet Hair Salon, each being over one and responsible for what goes in and comes out. Still, as Dorian said earlier, I can't figure why Envy ain't take the deal and then give us our respective roles."

Still remaining silent, I waited for the situation to be grasped. I knew who would get it first 'cause his eyes never left me during the entire conversation.

"You don't have to figure it out because it was already said," Michael commented, getting everybody's attention. "When D-Wild said why he assumed Envy brought him here in the first place. To have a meeting with her business partners. She knew who would be here and what she wanted done. She's the bank, and we work for her, but she trusts us as equals. Just think about it for a second."

"I get it," Dorian said again, being the first to catch on. "At least, I get the concept. When she got popped for that bullshit, she left Kyle in charge of the business but told us to continue handling business like she wasn't gone. She knew we ain't gon' crack under pressure, and if she gives us a job, it's as good as gold that we gon' be on our suit and tie shit."

"Now that we got that out of the way, and I see we all on the same page," I said, breaking my silence and bringing my attention to D-Wild. "Derek, you got yourself a deal. We ready whenever you can supply us with what we need."

"You really brought me here to show me how much of a Boss Bitch you are?" D-Wild questioned.

"Check," I responded simply.

"You brought me here to face your team, to see the mental strength that rides with you?" D-Wild asked, catching the chess reference.

"Check," my response was again simple.

"Your mind was already made up, but you wanted me to present it and, at the same time, make me work for what I presumed should be an easy, no-brainer of a choice?"

"Checkmate," I responded with a smile.

D-Wild smiled in response and left it at that.

"If we done with that," Michael said with a knowing look. "You gon' tell us who and why was the reason you was put up on murder charges?"

Leave it to Michael to bring it back to the light. Even though I figured he already knew enough about the problem, this confirmed it.

Everybody looked at me, waiting for the answer to the question since there wasn't any more money business to discuss at the moment.

With my answer, events were going to happen without an order to do so. So, I got myself ready for it as I began to answer.

CHAPTER FIVE

As I pulled away from the Diamond House, with D-Wild in the passenger seat beside me, I knew I left everyone stunned when I gave them the details of what happened and the history behind the ones who put me on the chopping block. What really left them with expressions of disbelief was the response to what I wanted to do about it.

Nothing.

I already knew Dorian wouldn't listen to the reason, so I addressed Kyle and Michael with my reason for my response. Knowing Dorian wouldn't listen meant Calvin wouldn't listen, but getting Kyle and Michael on the same page could clear things up and bring another view.

I ran a business, and those in my inner circle were a part of my business as a whole. For me to allow them to do something that could lead to legal ramifications, it could put my business in jeopardy.

That was a negative.

The example was shown when I got put on ice. The only reason I didn't go for bail was so the state didn't go digging into my business, believing I profited from a murder they thought I did. The way I got my businesses started was played as if my parents gave me the upstart money. Still, if the state dug around, they would see that I brought an excess amount of money that was tax-free. I didn't need that type of attention in my finances when I was trying to build a juggernaut of an empire. Everyone with me was under contract one way or another, so to put their self in legal jeopardy...

My point exactly.

So, I needed everybody to chill and leave something I already beat legally alone until further notice. I never said I wasn't coming back to it, just not right now, and perfectly planned.

"How do you view my decision?" I asked D-Wild since he remained quiet throughout the whole subject at the club.

"As a suit and tie nigga?" D-Wild responded with a chuckle. "Or a G from the street nigga?"

"Seeing as you present yourself as both a suit and tie and G from the street nigga," I countered seriously. "Put them together, or give me your view on how you feel."

"As a G from the street on his suit and tie shit," he began with a look of concentrated thought, "I understand your position perfectly. Now, let me give you my personal outlook as a whole."

He paused, waiting to see if I would interrupt him, then continued.

"Being as you are a businesswoman and still part of the streets means that you have built a mafia mentality. Right now, your shit is in straight business mode, and that's respected 'cause you always have to take business into account when making decisions of this magnitude," he voiced, gaining traction. "Now, your business wasn't threatened from a business competitor or even from a business point of view. Your business was threatened by the streets on a more personal note. So, me personally, I would put the suit and tie nigga on ice, let the street nigga deal with the problem, orchestrate the solution, then get back on my suit and tie shit until that street shit is needed again."

Before I could open my mouth, he continued again.

"Seeing as I haven't been put in that position yet, and I'm seeing your problem as my personal problem, I know eventually that's how I would have to handle it if it ever goes like this for me," D-Wild finished seriously. "That's me putting myself into your shoes.

Knowledge is that possession that no misfortune can destroy, no authority can revoke, and no enemy can control. This makes knowledge the greatest of all freedoms. When someone gives out jewels of knowledge, even though I'm a Boss Bitch in my own right, you take notice and become wiser.

The man, 'cause I can't call him a nigga no more, just revealed his value as a man of thought and thinking ability. He read the situation for what it was, put himself in the position of the situation, and gave a beautiful view on how he would handle the solution for the situation.

We remained in silence for the rest of the drive until I pulled into his driveway. That was when I expected D-Wild to go back all playful again, and I'd have to slow him down again.

"I know you got a lot on your mind, so check this out," D-Wild said, to my surprise. "Take these two blunts," he instructed after pulling out his cigar box and handing it to me," Take a nice hot bubble bath and let your mind wrap around everything around you without distraction. Call me if you need anything."

Without waiting for a response, he started to get out of the car before I stopped him. I had made my mind up about him on the drive home.

"Look, change clothes and come over to my house," I told him. "Call me when you get to my door so I can meet you there."

"Alright," he responded as he got out and closed his door.

****

While waiting on D-Wild's call, I opted to wear my sexy red nightgown, made of silk, with the matching robe. I didn't put on a bra, but I did put on a nice red lace Victoria's Secret g-string. As I reached for my fragrant lotion, my cell phone rang with Kelly Rowland's "Motivation" ringtone. I hit two buttons on the screen to answer.

"Yeah?" I answered the line.

"I'm walking up to your door now," D-Wild responded on the other end.

"Come in and make yourself comfortable," I replied,

thinking of his reaction with a smile. "The door is open. Just lock it behind you. Fix us some drinks, too."

"Alright," was all he said as I ended the call.

I lotioned my legs down with the lavender fragrance lotion. Done with that, I grabbed the two blunts D-Wild gave me before he got out of my car and headed to the front.

Ladies and gentlemen of the jury, before you judge me for my actions, let me explain them. Every woman who proclaims to be a boss should be proud of this boss move, as well as every man who wants a woman who thinks like a boss and doesn't sell herself lower than her value.

We all figured it would get to this point. However, as a boss and a woman, the point to get here had to be on my time, on my terms, and with my blessing. I proved that I don't need a man for my rise to the top but would take a partner willing to work with me. Now that the understanding was on equal ground and standing, I could allow myself to enjoy the pleasures I had denied myself. In this case, I could enjoy the long-awaited moment that I had wanted since I found out what it was.

Yeah, I had dudes every now and then, but a man my speed and caliber? A boss?

Not even close.

So, you'd have to forgive me if my expectations have been met in terms of the thinking ability and character of a true boss. The money didn't count 'cause money don't make a boss; a boss makes money. So, even if his finances wasn't on the level, the way he handled himself and carried himself today would have shown me enough potential to give him a play at the crown of being my king.

As I ran this through my mind, I exited the hallway, finding D-Wild sitting on the couch with a drink in his hand. He didn't notice me because his back was to me with the way the couch was set. I made my way to the kitchen before I made a subtle noise to get his attention and let him know I was in the room.

"What's up, Envy?" D-Wild questioned as he got up.

He was wearing sweatpants and a muscle shirt. He must have took me at my word 'cause his shoes were off, and I saw black socks on his feet.

The man was sexy as hell to me!

"I thought we might continue and conclude our business discussion from earlier," I said as I fixed myself a glass of Ciroc Apple on ice. "Now, we can get deeper into the subject without the worry of rush. Unless you have somewhere you need to be, that is?"

I could feel his eyes watching me, so I continued to fix my drink without turning around.

"Nah, ma, ain't nothing important set up for me anytime soon," he said with a hint of something to his voice. "If it ain't an emergency, it can wait. You got my undivided attention for as long as you want and/or need it."

Turning around, I saw the fire in his eyes that spoke volumes about what he could do to my body if I only let him have the opportunity.

"Can I be honest with you, Derek?" I asked, ready to show my hand.

"If you can't be real to me, you can't be real for me, and

I'm hoping you always remain real with me," he answered seriously yet playfully.

"I need you to show me how you treat your queen as a king," I responded, then sipped from my glass. "I need you to treat me as you see me and as the woman you plan to keep."

"Listen, ma, when I crank this car up, there ain't gon' be no pulling over so you can get out," D-Wild said, coming around the counter into the kitchen as he answered. "I'm going all in at top speed and leaving everything in the rearview. So, I need you to be sure about what you saying to me."

"Derek, my mind was made up when you first opened your mouth, and I heard you speak," I reassured him of my seriousness. "I just needed to show you what I had to offer and what you was going to receive by getting me. I'm my own woman, and I'll forever be independent. So, don't even conceive the notion that because of where we going with this, you'll be able to control me. Even in the bedroom, I'm untamed."

Standing in front of me, D-Wild reached for my hand and began to speak. Him holding my hand felt as natural as two lovers who had been together for ten plus years.

"Envy, I don't ever want you to change your way of hustle or the way that you control it in a boss fashion. That's what draws me to you as a man. I don't have to worry about if you can take care of yourself or not because it's overstood that you can handle yourself just as well and even better than some niggas I know." He said with a hint of a smile. "Now, the bedroom, on the other hand, you can't blame me for attempting to tame you. I know you have the same goal to tame this wild bull. Now, let me give you what you been asking for."

D-Wild led me by hand back to the couch with that Boss essence just dripping off of him in waves. Anticipation took over, and my juices started flowing just from watching him walk.

"I hope you don't mind that I took the time to Bluetooth my phone to your stereo system." He spoke, sitting me down on the couch and then reaching for his phone. "I wasn't expecting this since you slowed me down earlier, but I was going to give us a little background music for our discussion.

"Do your thing, baby boy," I responded as Ginuwine's "So Anxious" came through the surround sound system. "I told you what I needed from you. Trust me, if I ain't feeling it, I'll treat it like a business meeting gon' bad and end it."

As a response, D-Wild took off his muscle shirt, revealing that chiseled physique built for war and sex. With my drink still in my hand, I had to take a sip to keep myself from leaving my mouth hanging and drooling over myself.

Listening to Ginuwine sing about being anxious and watching D-Wild had me impatient for his touch. Every movement made a muscle jump and got me wetter as he took his time. That was when I noticed he didn't have on any underwear. Every woman knew when they saw that V on a man's body that goes from waist on down, without anything blocking it, was the sexiest shit. Especially when the man was muscular and fit. D-Wild had an eight-pack ab set that led to his V, which showed promise of what was to come.

When he kneeled in front of me, he took my drink out of my hand and downed the last before he sat it on the table behind him.

"I hope you ready, baby girl," he said seductively as he faced me again. "I'm gon' show you how you were supposed to have already been treated royally."

Before I could say a word, he leaned in to kiss me. Whenever our lips touched, we melted into each other with such familiarity that I didn't want to come up for air. His body was strong on mine, but he was gentle.

"Derek," I moaned when our kiss broke.

"I got you like All State," D-Wild spoke sexily before he drowned me with another powerful kiss.

I wanted him to tear that stupid robe I put on off of me. I was ready, but he kept me waiting in torture.

As if reading my mind, I felt the robe slide from my shoulders and rewarded him by throwing my legs around his waist. He immediately broke the kiss and separated my legs while simultaneously pulling me to the edge of the couch.

I was so caught up that I didn't hear what he said before my nightgown went over my head, and his lips locked onto one of my breasts, bringing a hiss and moan out of me. Licking and sucking me, he pinched and rolled the other between his fingers. When the one nipple was standing at attention, he switched sides and continued to pleasure me with only his mouth and hands.

When he left my breast and began kissing his way down, it took everything for me not to orgasm right on the spot. He stopped at my navel and gave it some attention, which had me screaming and squirming. Getting to my panty line, he licked along the edges, not even bothering to remove them. With that, my eyes closed.

"Ooh, yes!" I moaned when he nibbled, licked, and sucked my inner thigh right next to my wet box. "Do it just like that!"

When he grazed my clit, moving to my other inner thigh, I almost collapsed. When he locked onto me again, a shiver went up my spine that made my back arch so deep that I had to grip the couch cushions.

"Oh my god!" was all I could say when he began to lick me through my g-string as Musiq Soulchild's "Love" began to play.

His mouth did its dance of pleasure, and I knew he could taste my juices through the lace. Without using his hands, his tongue slid under my panties and licked the fold all the way up to my pearl tongue, bringing me to an earth-shattering orgasm. When his tips locked onto my pearl, a second orgasm took me before the first was anywhere near done.

"Oh shit! Oh shit! Ooh shit! Right there, shit!" I moaned in ecstasy, giving him a nod that he was doing his best shit and I didn't want him to stop.

All I got in return was a muffled "mmmhmm" and chuckle.

When the last wave of the orgasms was ridden out, he unlatched from my pearl and gave me a final lick before looking up at me. Without a word but a huge smile, he began sliding my panties off. I immediately brought my legs up and lifted them straight into the air. When the g-string was off, I let my legs split open so he could get a good look at this boss pussy he just got through licking.

"Beautiful, just beautiful. Delicious, too," D-Wild said with a smile and licking his lips. "I could do that all night until I put you in a coma."

"I'll have to take you up on that sometime in the future," I responded, bringing my legs down.

As if reading my mind, he stood up. I don't know when he came out of his sweatpants, but in front of my face was the most beautiful piece of meat on a man I had ever seen. The color of the Snickers, with a beautiful dark pink head, looked to be a good nine and a half to ten and a half inches.

I stood up, reaching for it. When I got a hold of it, it was warm, hard, and ready.

"Sit down," I instructed. "I'm bout to put you inside this treasure and give you a special thank you for the royal treatment."

Now, I could have gave him some boss head, but my treasure needed him to be inside me right then and there. Besides, there was always the next session I could torture him with this boss head game.

When he complied with my request and was seated, I straddled him, letting his wood feel my wetness as I went in for a kiss. Tasting my own juices turns me on for some reason.

When D-Wild gripped my ass with his strong hands, I lifted myself up, reaching down to put him in my wetness. Slowly lowering myself down onto his head and feeling his thickness, my treasure opened, tightly gripping him. I stopped right on his head and slowly went up and down, not allowing his full length into me. Working up and down and gradually sinking lower on every down motion, when I finally got the full length of him in me, I sat there and worked my muscles around him.

"Damn, Envy!" he moaned, still gripping my ass. "This pussy is one of a fucking kind!"

In response, I threw my elbows on his shoulders and put my hands on top of his head as I kissed him deep and started riding him. I let myself rise slowly, close to him coming out of me, before sliding back down, letting my lower body dance to the music that was playing.

"This some good dick, boy!" I moaned, breaking the kiss but not the rhythm of my ride. "Damn, ooh shit, this some good dick!"

D-Wild started going thrust for thrust with me, making it feel as if I had a horse under me I was riding.

"I'm bout to cum!" I moaned, "Derek, I'm bout to cum."

As if hearing his name could do it, he went wild under me, gripping my ass and meeting on my way down, bringing me closer to that big orgasm every woman dreams of.

"I'm cumming! Fuck! I'm cumming!" I screamed and moaned and was treated to more thrusts. Then another orgasm hit behind that one. Not losing momentum, our rhythm kept going, and yet another orgasm hit me, taking me to the edge. The orgasm was so toe-curling and mindblowing that I don't know how D-Wild ended up on top of me, still working his stroke game and bringing me to another orgasm.

"You better work, D-Wild!" I moaned in wonderful

pleasure. "Dig! Show me why they call you D-Wild!"

That was when he switched gears and started rolling his whole body in the motion of a wave, long stroking for what he was worth.

"Fuck, I'm bout to come, Envy!" he moaned, never losing stride.

"You better not stop! You better not stop!" I moaned back.

The pressure that was building came to a peak, and the strongest orgasm I ever felt rocked me hard. I gripped my treasure around D-Wild, and he growled.

"I'm cumming!" he moaned, pounding.

He rode the wave of his orgasm until all he could do was shake. I rode mine out with him until he became still. J. Holiday's "Bed" decided to come on over the speakers, and I was extremely satisfied with the moment.

After listening to J. Holiday, Trey Songz's voice took over with "Neighbors Know My Name," and I was ready for round two. D-Wild must have felt the same 'cause he chose that moment to speak into my ear.

"Round two in the bedroom?" he said, licking my ear and sending a shiver through me.

"Carry me," I responded simply.

"Yes, ma'am," he said, lifting me with him. "That will be done."

CHAPTER SIX

In the coming weeks, me and D-Wild became in sync. He supplied Dorian with the products we wanted to distribute. Dorian, Michael, and Calvin put the products in the trap spots and onto the streets. Kyle got his portion and split it among the Diamond House, which he put Vanessa in charge of; Diamond Escorts, which he put Kayla in charge of; and The Red Carpet, which he gave Jordan the run of. We were all getting settled, but I never forgot about Jazmine.

Each week, I put a Ben Frank on her books and sent her a couple lines. I also stayed in touch with her lawyer so I could be updated on her status. Like I said, when I put my stamp on something, it's written in stone. All a person has in this world that's truly there is their word. So, you stand by that shit. As a boss, your words have to be put into action, or you don't get the respect for your word. If you say that, mean that, and make sure you represent that, 'cause your word is an extension of you.

So, when I got a call and didn't know the number, imagine my surprise when I heard Jazmine speak.

"Damn, bitch, you finally decided to hit a bitch up," I answered her. "I thought I was being a trick waiting on your call."

"Girl, please! Never dat," Jazmine responded. "You know how it is in here."

"Yeah, so talk to me," I said as I pulled into my driveway.

I had errands to run earlier and had decided to drive the Audi to keep a semi-low profile. The 745 was for when I was feeling myself.

"Well, I talked to Timberly today about my case," she began. "You know she like to pop up on a bitch to deliver her news."

"Yeah," I acknowledged, anxious to hear what happened.

She stayed quiet for a second before she continued.

"Bitch, I get out tomorrow, girl!" she said excitedly. "The DA fucked up and didn't have everything they said they did. I don't know exactly what happened, but when Timberly told the DA she was ready for trial, the DA tried to 42 fake her. Remember, I been here for damn near a year, so they had to come on with it. So, when the DA hesitated, she went to the judge and explained the situation."

I waited for her to keep going, happy for her.

"He dismissed my shit right then and there," she said slowly. "The only reason I ain't getting out today is because I did a plea bargain on the unauthorized use of a motor vehicle for 10 months. I'll have time served tomorrow without leaving the city!"

"Call me so I can pick you up. I got a surprise for you." I told her, already thinking of a gift for her. "When you see Jones, tell her what's up and tell her she needs to call a bitch, too."

"Aight, girl!" Jazmine responded. "See you tomorrow. And thank you for not being one of them fake ass hoes that try to sell a bitch dreams."

"Bitch bye!" I said, ending the call.

Jazmine getting out soon worked out perfectly. See, I had enough time to think and wanted Jazmine to be part of my team. I know she ain't no groupie, so I'd have to show her the benefits of fucking with a Boss Bitch.

To do that, I decided to get her a car. Since I wanted to get a new vehicle anyway, I just decided to give her the Audi. So I would have to take it to a car wash and get a full detail job done on it.

Reversing back out of my driveway, I made my way to the car wash in Da Haven off Shelby Drive. A full detail only cost you 20-25 dollars, and they always did a good job. It also gave me time to find myself a replacement car--which I already decided would be a Lexus IS250. The year model was up for grabs. It would come down to availability.

I passed D-Wild's Magnum on the way out of the neighborhood and figured I could expect his call in a few moments. We didn't have anything planned for tonight, but he liked to play cat-and-mouse games with me. We stayed in a chess battle of wits keeping each other sharp, not wanting our senses dulled for any reason.

D-Wild's ringtone blared from my phone's speaker, not

letting me down.

"What's up, baby boy?" I answered the phone.

"If I was insecure, I would think you was running away from me," he responded with a chuckle. "Since I'm not insecure, what you got planned for tonight?"

"Well, right now, I need to find a new car after I get this one detailed," I explained sweetly. "I may need your help picking it up, and after that, I'm free."

"Anything specific in mind, car-wise?" he asked. "I can be another set of eyes for you."

"A Lexus IS 250, 2008 and up," I answered. "Good condition with the motor where I won't have to put too much money into it."

"Anything else?" he asked.

"JJ's," I responded. "Get the 10-piece and fries with a drink. I want to relax tonight. Big day tomorrow."

"Got you. I'll get back with you later," D-Wild said. "Bye."

"Bye," I said, ending the call.

Ten minutes later, I was watching the Audi get its special treatment as I searched for my car online. I came up with three but had to delete them because the mileage on them was too high for the prices they were asking.

I got a text alert from D-Wild saying he found me a 2008 IS 250 with 30,000 miles for 11,00 dollars. He also shot me pictures from different angles and a description to go with it. It was a midnight blue with light tint. Everything inside was factory, same with the rims.

I texted him back that I wanted to see it in person. When he responded it could be arranged, I knew he must have known the person selling the car. So, I asked if he could tell me where I would be going. He texted back that I would be going to Germantown, where a used car lot was located.

I let it go at that. If the car was drivable, I would be sending it to one of Papi's friends to have the custom work done on it. Until then, I would need a rental 'cause I didn't want to burn my 745 up. I could deal with that after I picked up Jazmine, though.

Bringing my attention from my phone, I was just in time to notice Tasha and Ivy walking up on me with mugs on their faces. Knowing I had my equalizer with me, I didn't even move. I just watched them approach.

"Look who it is, T," Ivy said as she stepped closer. "Is it the too-good-for-the-hood bitch Envy?"

"Nah, that can't be Envy," Tasha said with an exaggerated look on her face. "Not after she dissed us hood bitches with that 'Boss Bitch' talk."

"Oh, but it is I!" I said mockingly. "I'm just in the hood as usual, but this time, I'm getting a gift ready for a real stand-up bitch. Not a rat bitch!"

That got the car wash's attention and brought heat to Tasha and Envy's faces.

"So, let me ask you both something, in the hood where the code is law in the streets!" I started, standing up and getting louder. "How did it feel to snitch on a Boss Bitch 'cause you hoes are haters?! How does it feel to snitch on somebody that was your day one?! Oh, and how does it feel to know that even though you snitched, a Boss Bitch is still on top?!"

"Bitch, you got us fucked up!" Ivy screamed.

"No, I got you fucked right, with y'all names in black and white as state evidence against me!" I said, revealing the .380 in my hand. "So, I suggest you hoes fall back 'cause I got every right to bust you two bitches in the ass!"

Not even pressed, I sat down, covered my hand back up with my purse, and continued to stare them down.

"That's how we doing it?" Ivy asked like she was a true gangsta. "Cause that's the last time a gun gon' be pointed at me on your behalf!"

"And what you bitches gone do?!" a voice shouted from behind me. "Cause if you fucking with Envy, you got a mothafuckin' problem that's bout to get worse."

From the accent in the chick's voice, I knew that it had to be Kayla with her ready-for-war ass. Texas bitches.

"How bout I beat both you hoes asses?!" Kayla said, walking around into my view in boy shorts, a sports bra, and tennis shoes. "Line that shit up one at a time! Step right on up, 'cause you are the next contestant on the Price is Right! Tell 'em what they won, Envy!"

With the car wash as the audience, and the stage set, like a Boss Bitch supposed to, I crossed my legs in a professional fashion and broke into an onward winning smile.

Colgate would be proud.

"You won an expense-paid trip to one of Memphis's most pristine medical facilities, in whichever manner you chose," I said, giving a show. "The trip will be taken by ambulance or helicopter, but it won't be by limousine. All this could be yours if the price is right!"

Seeing as they were being clowned in front of a live hood

audience, Tasha decided to try her luck. Noticing Tasha move, Ivy made a play to jump in.

Before I could move, Kayla ducked Tasha's swing, pushed her to the side, and hit Ivy with an elegant textbook two-piece combo that sat her on her ass, struck and stunned. Without hesitation, she turned back to Tasha, who was already swinging with everything she had in one punch. Kayla tried to block and duck all at once. When Tasha connected, she hit Kayla's guard while she was ducking down, which rocked Kayla enough for Tasha to get up for another swing.

I don't know if Kayla expected to be rocked or just rolled with the punch, but whichever it was, Kayla was cocked and locked with the right like a shotgun and let it go aiming for Tasha's chin. When she connected with Tasha's chin, the sound was so meaty and loud that I cringed and heard a collective "ooh!" from around the car wash. Tasha's head went back, and you know the saying: "Wherever the head goes, the body will follow."

Kayla turned to Ivy, who was just standing up, and watched her next move. Ivy noticed Tasha on the ground and looked at Kayla with her mind made up. She charged in, going for the old hair pull. Kayla sidestepped and launched a night hook that lifted Ivy off of her feet, flatlining her in the air.

Four punches, and I didn't even have to pull my .380 or jump in. Without a care in the world, Kayla sat beside me and looked at her hands, surveying the damage that was done.

"These bitches made me break a nail!" Kayla shouted,

staring at them while they were still on the ground. "I just got these hoes done not even thirty minutes ago!"

All I could do was sit there dumbfounded at the show Kayla just put on. Yeah, Kyle gave me her credentials, but this was a firsthand look at what she was capable of.

"What?" she asked innocently.

"Excuse me, ladies," some nice-looking dude said, getting our attention. "I overheard you say that you broke a nail. Allow me to pay to get them redone."

Dude was every bit of six feet, or better, with a nice build. He had his hair in a Caesar cut with deep waves rolling into his caramel skin. Small diamonds adorned both ears. Knowing my labels, he wore a red and black short-sleeved Prada sweater, revealing intricate tattoos on his arms. He wore a Patek Philippe watch with a red band and a white gold pinky ring with the dollar sign encrusted in diamonds. He had on a pair of red Prada slacks and a belt matching the sweater. On his feet, to bring it all home, were a pair of black Prada shoes.

Dude was clean and screamed money. Plus, he was hot.

"What's your name, honey?" Kayla asked him.

"Aaron, but everybody calls me A1," he responded. "And you?"

"I'm Kayla, and this is my girl Envy." Kayla introduced us both.

His eyes flicked in recognition, but I knew I never met dude before. It put me on edge a little until he spoke.

"Please don't tell me you the same Envy that D-Wild been speaking highly of," he said with a true smile.

"One and the same, most likely," I responded.

"Hold that thought," Al said, bringing his attention back to Kayla. "Kayla, I was being sincere when I offered to pay to get your nails redone."

Before she could answer, both Tasha and Ivy began getting to their feet. Noticing our attention shifted, Al turned to them.

"You two ratchet ass chicken head hoes," Al said loud and clear, "get y'all snitch asses out of here! Catch ghost before some hood justice take place out here on your asses! I know the info on you hoes, and I don't like snakes!"

Not even checking to see if they obeyed his command, Al turned his attention back to Kayla, waiting for a response.

Letting Kayla have her moment, I pulled my phone out to call D-Wild to inform him on the situation before it got out by way of hood news.

"What's up, girl?" he answered on the second ring.

"You know Aaron or Al by any chance?" I asked him.

"Yeah, that's my guy. Why?" he responded.

"He right here hitting on my girl, shooting his shot," I remarked.

"Oh, okay," he said. "He a good dude for what it's worth coming from me. He ain't got nobody right now if that's what you're trying to find out."

"Not really, but it's good to know," I said. Then I went on to give him the low down on what transpired at the car wash.

D-Wild kept laughing and cutting me off, wanting me to repeat certain shit like the "Price Is Right" stunt we pulled. When I got to the part about Kayla shutting down the car wash in four punches, he said he hoped somebody recorded the whole display so he could see it from start to finish. I told him that my name was said, and it would most likely get to me first.

"Hold on for a second," I told D-Wild, thinking of something. "Excuse me, A1. Would you have, by chance, recorded what happened out here?"

"I didn't even…" A1 said, looking wounded, then busted into a smile. "I'm from the hood, ma, and we love to see a good fight. Of course, I did."

"Boy, you something else!" I said with a smile. "Could you send D-Wild a copy so he can stop laughing in my ear every time he hear something funny to him?"

"You got him on the line?" he asked. "Can I holla at him real quick?"

While he talked to D-Wild, Kayla explained how she rolled up on me in the first place. She really wanted to see if some hood shit was popping off at the car wash. Getting out of her car, she heard my name and my voice, putting her on alert and ready. She even witnessed me showing my pistol, so when the threat was made, she decided to make her presence felt. You know the rest.

I was happy and relieved that she showed up but, at the same time, upset. 'Cause all the while I was checking them hoes, I was itching for them bitches to run up on me so I could air their ass out. I expressed that to Kayla, who only told me she was happy she had me to my bullets.

With my mind made up, I asked her if she would ride with me to pick up Jazmine the next day. She accepted with a shrug of her shoulders and asked when and where to meet her. Since the house that Diamond Escorts was operating out of was close to her on the way to my destination, we agreed to meet there.

"D-Wild told me to let you know that he was on the way to the used car lot and to meet him there when you was done here." A1 relayed the message, handing me my phone. "He also said stay a Boss Bitch, not a False Bitch."

All I could do was smile as A1 turned his attention back to Kayla, who accepted his offer and invited him to link up at the nail shop up the street when his car was done being detailed. He pointed at an old school Cadillac Eldorado that looked like something them Texas boys out of Houston be talking bout and said he was already finished.

When I pulled into the car wash, I noticed the candy apple red masterpiece, with the chrome grill and woman, sitting on 84's and white wall tires. When I asked where he was from, he said he was from Da Haven. He explained that since his parents was separated, during the school year, he would stay with his mom, but during the summer vacations, he would spend time with his pops in Houston.

Kayla, being out of the Third Ward area of Houston, went with the connection of the city, and they dove right into conversation, getting familiar with each other.

Making that my cue, I zoned out and calculated the next steps to solidify my place in the game. Most people would say I should be content with what I had and ride out my success. I wasn't born and bred to be comfortable with just anything, especially when you're in the building process of your dreams. Plus, the Boss Bitch that I was needed to make sure that I left a top-notch legacy behind with the dynasty I was working to create. Anything else would be uncivilized for a business professional who worked as hard as I have, trying to make a name for themselves under the shadow of parents who dominated the game and left their mark.

No one person had ever understood the value of how I came to name my business. Platinum is one of the most expensive metals in the world, whereas diamonds are the most expensive jewel in the world, and the red carpet is where you see these come together in complete elegance. Diamond House and Diamond Escorts were the jewels, showing value as they shone on the red-carpet events. But, it was Platinum Services, which was the metal that had the jewels embedded in it, holding them together so they could shine bright as one.

"Envy," Kayla said, snapping me out of my thoughts. "Girl, your whip ready. Whatever you was thinking bout just now had you gone!"

"Just thinking bout a dollar, as usual," I responded. "Alright, girl, I'll see you tomorrow. Nice meeting you, A1."

"Bye, girl," Kayla responded back.

"Nice meeting you, too," A1 said, "Try to stay out of trouble."

Reaching the Audi, I had a thought about Tasha and Ivy, but I filed it away for later thinking. Plus, they would get what they had coming.

****

Making it to the used car lot in Germantown, my hopes weren't at their best that the Lexus would be worth it. I spotted D-Wild's Magnum as I pulled into the lot and made my way to park by him. Getting closer, that was when I noticed the car I was looking for.

At first glance, the car looked to be in damn good condition, but we all know that looks can be deceiving. I knew I needed to see the rest of the car, and then I would know how much money I would need to put into it. It would also let me know if I'd try to negotiate a lower price or take it as is. Pulling into the space beside D-Wild's car, I got a text telling me to go ahead and check out the car. So, I turned off my shit and got out to do just that.

I could tell it had just been washed by the shine of the tires. Walking around the car, I didn't see any dents or defects in the paint. The tint was professionally done, too. Satisfied that all I would do was change the paint color and put new rims on it, I opened the car door to see the interior. Without looking, my mind was made up for putting in another sound system. The blue leather did it for me. It was staying. I would add just a touch of wood grain on the dash, steering wheel, doors, and consoles, but for the most part, I was sold on the Lexus. Screens in the headrests were a must, as well as one coming out of the dash. I pushed the bottom for the trunk and stood up.

I closed the doors, ready to see the trunk. Getting it to open and close by itself was on my list. Opening the trunk, I saw the potential for my taste. Four 15" kickers in a custom tinted fiberglass box and three 2500x Sony amps to power them. I'd trade the inside speakers for 6" x 9" Sony's in the doors.

"What you think?" D-Wild's voice came from behind me.

"I still ain't looked at the engine yet, but so far, so good," I responded, not bothering to turn around. "I already got a picture of what I want to do to it if I get though."

Closing the trunk, I make my way back to the driver's door to hit the hood latch.

Doing that and getting to the hood, I looked back and noticed an older cat standing with D-Wild. Had to be the owner. I turned my attention back to the hood and opened it up. Everything looked okay.

"D-Wild, can you start it for me?" I asked, not looking up, focused on what I was seeing. I remembered the first time I ever drove one of these exact-year models and wanted to compare what I remembered to what I was seeing and about to hear.

D-Wild got to the driver's seat and brought the car to life the next second without a hitch. Listening for a minute, my mind was made up. They didn't know it yet.

"Alright, you can cut her off," I called out to D-Wild.

The older cat just stood there, quietly watching my reactions.

"You the owner?" I asked him, making eye contact.

"Yeah, so what you think?" he responded.

I remained quiet for a minute, gauging how to respond when D-Wild asked me a question.

"How much you think you putting into it if you take it?" D-Wild asked, knowing my answer would set the stage for my deal attempt.

"1,200 for the paint, 5-600 on the sound system, couple hundred on the touch-up on the interior, maybe 5 tops, 3 plus grand on rim, tires, and breaks, and a couple hundred for an automatic trunk," I answered, giving the numbers. "Close to six grand or better. Not including the engine if any tweaks need to be done to it."

"So?" D-Wild prompted.

"I'd buy it for 9,500 with a check right now," I said bluntly, looking at the owner.

"10.5," he countered.

"I'll meet you in the middle with 10, and you keep my inspection sticker ready after I get her fired up," I said, trying to close the deal at the price I wanted to pay in the first place.

"You got a deal," he said to me, then looked at D-Wild. "You wasn't lying about her at all. She's a keeper."

D-Wild laughed. "I know it, Unc!"

"Come on in so we can get this paperwork done, and you go on about your business." The owner, who I now knew was D-Wild's uncle, said.

"We can do all the paperwork, but I want to pick it up tomorrow afternoon sometime," I said as we went towards the building.

"It'll be my pleasure, Ms. Woman!" D-Wild's uncle responded happily.

Two more moves to make, and I would be good.

The first move would be to Papi's friend, Tito, to let him

know I had a car I wanted him to custom for me and give him the details. The second would be tomorrow to Enterprise Car Rental after Tito told me how long he would take.

Now, all I had to do was get my sales pitch ready for Jazmine and let her watch all the moves I made after I picked her up.

CHAPTER SEVEN

After getting the whole story from D-Wild on how he and his Uncle Leroy plotted on how to counter my reaction and negotiation, they decided that if his uncle was to make a sale to me, then he would have to let me decide my price. Then, we would get to a number meeting in the middle. Now, sitting on my couch with my legs over D-Wild's lap as he massaged my feet, I was watching the posted video of the car wash incident.

Social media at its finest.

The caption under the video said, "Two-on-one handicap turns to a one-on-two mismatch." My name was tagged on the video, as were others. The shit went viral on a number of social media sites: Facebook, Instagram, Tango, ooVoo, Kik, YouTube, and Twitter.

Yes, I had accounts in all of them, with followers and friends to go with them. So, I got all the alerts once my name was mentioned. I didn't know how to feel about that. I only noticed because my name was said, but once they found out who she was, Kayla would be the one who became famous. So, what I did was send the video and a text to Kyle, telling him to get at me ASAP PDQ (As Soon As Possible Pretty Damn Quick).

My mind, trying to formulate what would happen next, was at a standstill for the simple fact that by Tasha and Ivy being embarrassed at the car wash in Da Haven, anything could happen from here on out. I never told Kayla who the hoes were, but I assumed she figured it out by the conversation.

"Snap out of it, Envy," D-Wild said, squeezing my foot. "You been zoned out since we got here so much I'm thinking you might be planning a murder."

If only he knew how much on point he was with that analysis.

"I just know how them hoes are," I explained, keeping my thoughts to myself for the moment. "I rocked with them bitches damn near my whole hustle career, so I know they plotting something. You can't expect them not to have seen this video. Hell, they names tagged in the shit, too!"

"Them hoes ain't bout that life, E. If they know what's best for them, they'll find a quiet spot to sit and stay out the way," D-Wild commented.

"That's the problem right there. Don't underestimate these bitches. That was a lot of people's downfall when we started up together." I told him. "We ran through mothafuckas like wrecking balls through wood when we got played for soft. Tasha was the brawn, Ivy was the brains, and since I was the smallest, I had more to prove when shit popped off."

I sat back, still thinking, and continued.

"Me and Tasha always went head up sparring, getting our hands better and better. Not many could stand toe to toe with us, which is why my gear game in my face is minimum or non-existent." I explained. "For them to get done how they did, they gon' find some bitches they keep on reserve and start asking questions. Thing is, since I been split from them, I don't know who they got behind them and what power they holding."

D-Wild remained quiet, still massaging my feet.

My thoughts went back to the question that was asked weeks ago at the Diamond House.

What I'm gon' do about it?

I said nothing as an answer, but now I knew for a fact that something had to be done.

Rick Ross' "Hustlin" ringtone chose that moment to come from my phone.

"Yeah," I answered, knowing it was Kyle.

"First, when was this video taken?" he asked over the phone.

"This afternoon," I answered.

"Second, why am I just now finding out bout it?" he asked, sounding annoyed.

"As you can see, it was taken care of quickly and professionally," I answered back and countered with my own question. "Why you ain't tell me this bitch could throw down like that?"

"I told you all we do growing up is fight," he answered.

understanding no matter how insignificant they think, or feel it is.

Hint, my simple 'okay' to D-Wild's speech. Most bitches would have taken it offensively, but I was a Boss Bitch for real. He checked me on my attitude sure enough, but he never overstepped. He went "Boss Nigga" mode for his "Boss Bitch" to understand and gave it raw and uncut.

The shit turned me on.

"Okay?" he asked, registering that I wasn't going to argue.

"Yeah," I responded nonchalantly. "You're completely right, and I understand your position. If the shoe was on the other foot, I would do the same damn thing. Like you said, as a couple, we share problems, but we won't get in the other's way of dealing with it and will always be there as each other's back up like a Pitbull on a leash waiting for the "kill" command."

Checkmate.

****

D-Wild gave me the info telling me that Tasha and Ivy were both fucking with two dudes out of East Memphis in the Orange Mound area or Da Mound. The two dudes headed up a clique of niggas that called themselves "Orange Mound Money Gang." DiVinci and Capone, their real names, D-Wild knew from before he left for the Marines. Before he left, Orange Mound Money Gang was a group of up-and-coming niggas making names for themselves by hustling hard and blowing everything off the map that came between them and they money. Eventually, they got to the point where they took over Orange Mound without violence but with a monetary takeover. They supplied the drugs distributed in that area by themselves. They ran they shit mafia style and have been known to put hits out and had an army of niggas ready to put in work at a moment's call.

D-Wild, thinking ahead, put the word out that he was backing me and that we were together. To my surprise, D-Wild was the head of M.A.C. Mafia out of Oakhaven, where we was born, raised, and resided. I didn't put it together when he told me he was a M.A.C., a Man About Cash, at first because you rarely heard about M.A.C. Mafia. Everyone in the hood knew about it and even knew some of the members, but nobody knew who was at the top.

While D-Wild was away, all the money he sent back went to his family and M.A.C. Mafia to ensure the rise of the cause. He had his pops invest in stocks and bonds along with other legitimate businesses and had his second-in-command, A1, invest in M.A.C. Mafia. Without my knowing, when he found out that Dorian, Michael, and Calvin were a part of Da Haven's Black Haven Gorillas, he arranged a meeting with Dorian's oldest brother, Tony (aka Magic), who was the leader, and made a truce through the two crews, who never had beef before in the past.

On the other side of the coin, M.A.C. Mafia and Orange Mound Money Gang had a long-standing beef, back from when D-Wild, A1, DiVinci, and Capone were all still in high school.

"Get the fuck outta here!" I said, expressing my disappointment. "You can't be serious!"

"Hey, it ain't my fault they chicks was groupies!" D-Wild responded with a laugh. "When they seen me and A1 was bout money, they jumped. We ain't know they had niggas!"

"Would that have stopped you?" I asked, knowing the answer.

"Hell no!" he answered firmly. "Like we told them niggas when we found out. It wasn't our fault they hoes was bust downs!"

"No, you didn't!" I laughed loudly.

"Fucking right! That's when they decided to meet us after school one day and call us out." D-Wild continued animatedly. "They came to our head, in front of our school! Then had the audacity to have them hoes with them! Best believe I gave a show."

Looking at D-Wild, I understood why he had the name. Derek was wild.

"I told her if they was fighting for they honor, they was wasting they time 'cause them hoes ain't have none." He continued, "They ain't back down, so we beat they ass and sent them bout they way. After that, me and A1 fucked the hoes one more time and posted it on Instagram with the time and date attached, plus the caption saying, 'Orange Mound niggas got beat down behind them hoes.' I tagged they name along with the hoes."

He finished explaining that they had more run-ins after that, even after forming their respective cliques where M.A.C. Mafia came out on top each time. Reason being, M.A.C. Mafia had already been together for a few years before Orange Mound Money Gang. Then D-Wild went to the Marines on some grown folk shit. Serving his five-year obligation, he came back, and it seemed his beef really was my beef. So as fate had it, I got a problem with the hoes, and D-Wild got a problem with the niggas.

Rich Homie Quan's "Some Type of Way" ringtone emitted from D-Wild's phone. When he answered his phone, I chose that moment to make a call of my own. The phone was answered after three rings.

"What's good, boss?"

"I may need a favor from you, Cat Daddy," I stated bluntly, skipping pleasantries. "I got a little problem that may get out of hand."

I heard a mumble of conversation before I got a response.

Cat Daddy, his twin brother Money Mike, and they younger brother Sir Brit were three known pimps around the city, but nobody knew how lethal they were. They averaged 5'9"-5'10" in height and 190 or so in muscular weight. You would truly mistake them for being pretty boy pimpin' by their features. You rarely seen one without the others, even when they had they hoes with them. After getting to know them, they explained that they were doughboys and got money by any hustle necessary.

I found out what they meant when they showed up at the Diamond House in all black from head to toe. I just so happened to be there that night, and they spotted me. I didn't even know who they was until they got close. They came to air out a snitch that was supposed to testify on a client of theirs. They was going to get them right then and there until they seen me. Instead, they waited 'til they mark left and shot his car up in the parking lot. I got rid of my tapes that night, so I couldn't help the investigation, and I then put fresh tapes in and left. We been close ever since because they saw I was thorough.

"You called right on time 'cause we was planning on taking our hoes to Atlanta to pull in some bread and enjoy ourselves," Cat Daddy said back on the line. "You want to explain the problem to me, or you just want us to be on standby?"

I decided to give him the short version. The snitching, which I knew they hated with a passion, and the niggas behind them. I gave them permission to look into it and get as much info as they could but not to act at the moment.

"I understand small problems lead to big problems that become life-altering massive problems." Cat Daddy said. "We'll check shit out and get back to you. Call if you need us."

With that, he ended the call without waiting for a response. I looked at my phone and saw it was after eleven p.m. and looked at D-Wild.

He had an amused look on his face but remained silent.

"What?" I said with a smile of my own.

"Cat Daddy, huh?" he responded, still amused. "Next time you talk to him or his brothers, tell him 'Wild MAC Express' said what's gangsta."

"Okay, I'll do that," I agreed. "Now, can you put me to bed? Or do I have to do it myself?" By way of answer, he carried me to the bedroom and put me to bed like J. Holiday.

CHAPTER EIGHT

T he following morning, I was awakened by D-Wild telling me that he had to go take care of some business. I looked at the clock on the nightstand, and the time read 9:30 am. I didn't bother asking D-Wild any questions, seeing he was dressed in a suit and tie. So, I got up as he left to get myself together for the day.

After showering and knowing what was scheduled for the day, I dressed hood, classic casual, white Ralph Lauren polo shirt, Levi 501 jeans, and all-white low-top Reebok classics. The only things that screamed money on me were the JB Star Platinum diamond rings by Rafael on my right ring finger and left pinky finger, the custom platinum BVLGARI Roma watch with half-carat diamonds around the face, and the pink sapphire, diamond, and platinum earrings by Harry Winston. I also had a white Versace handbag with the shoulder strap, but unless you knew fashion, you couldn't tell.

As I was leaving out the door, my phone gave a generic ring, signaling the number wasn't locked into my phone.

"Hello?" I answered, expecting Jazmine to say she was headed out the door.

"Jazmine said you wanted me to call you, so I waited 'til my break," Brittney said, or should I say, C.O. Jones.

"Girl, yes!" I said, excited. "You never used my number, girl, and I'm trying to add some more money to my business."

"Lock my number in your phone, and I'll call when my shift over," she said with a laugh. "They already started the paperwork for your girl's release, too. Should be calling her down in like thirty to forty-five minutes."

"I know, I'm picking her up," I responded.

"Good, I might find a way for me to escort down," she said. "I'll hopefully see you then. I gotta go."

The line went dead, and I called Kayla to see where she was. She was already at Diamond Escorts waiting on me. Letting her know I was on my way, I got in the Audi and proceeded in that direction.

After picking up Kayla and making it to the jail thirty minutes later, we were still waiting for Jazmine to be released when I got a phone call that would change my attitude forever.

"Talk to me," I answered D-Wild's call.

"You should be getting another call saying that Diamond House is on fire, burning down at a rapid pace." D-Wild broke the news to me.

"Fuck you mean burning down?!" I yelled into the phone.

"Take a breath, ma," D-Wild said calmly. "The fire department is here already trying to get it under control."

"Let me call you back," I said, ending the call, not waiting for a response.

"Bitch, what's up?" Kayla asked as I speed-dialed Kyle.

"Somebody set Diamond House on fire," I responded heatedly.

Kayla immediately pulled out her phone to make a call.

"What's up, boss?" Kyle answered.

"Are you aware that Diamond House is on fire?" I asked him.

"Stop playing…"

"I'm not playing at all, Kyle!" I shouted. "Somebody set the bitch on fire, and I need you to get there to figure out what happened. Get Dorian and them to help you."

"Done," he answered simply and ended the call.

Looking up, I saw Jazmine standing outside, looking both ways with a disappointed look. So, I honked the horn and got her attention as I waved out the window. I then got out of the car and made my way to her, hoping I would see Brittney, too.

My mental attitude must have shown on my face because Jazmine stopped smiling and got a real serious look on her face. The change was so sudden that I had to force myself to smile.

"Naw, bitch," Jazmine called me out on it. "What's on your mind? I know I'm happy I just got out, but I know the world ain't stop for me."

"I'll tell you in the car," I remarked. "Did Jones walk you down?"

"Yeah, but we both ain't see you, so she went back in," she answered. "She said for you to be expecting her call later on."

"That's cool," I said, turning back to go to the car with Jazmine behind me. "Well, my day just got a little busier. So, instead of three stops, we now got four to make. Plus, get something to eat."

At the car, I saw that Kayla got into the backseat.

"This your shit?" Jazmine asked.

"For now," I answered cryptically.

As we got into the car, I introduced Kayla and Jazmine to each other. Not letting me slide, Jazmine went back to her question of what was up. I debated on how I should tell her and decided to give her all of it.

During the ride, I filled her in on what's been going on. The good, the bad, and the ugly. Everything that led up to today. The only thing was, I didn't tell her who was connected to who. By being connected to the streets, she was able to put a couple pieces of the puzzle together. That was why I wanted her on the squad.

When we pulled into the parking lot of Diamond House, my blood pressure skyrocketed to the moon. I gripped the steering wheel, and my knuckles started popping and turning red. I had to hold in a scream that I knew would be blood-curdling. I also knew I had to calm myself down before I exited the vehicle and be a show of strength, not showing any weakness. Kayla hopped out while I was composing myself.

I looked around and noticed D-Wild, Kyle, Dorian, Michael, and Calvin in a small circle off to the side, conversating, while Kayla, Vanessa, and Jordan stood in front of the smoking club. The fire had been put out completely before I pulled up. From looking at the club, you could tell that the inside was a hell of a mess that was going to cost me a pretty fucking penny to get repaired. What I really wanted to know, but already suspected, was who would fuck with my place of business, interfering with my financial income.

"Envy?" Jazmine asked a silent question beside me.

"I'm good," I respond. "Trust me, if I wasn't, I would be jumping to a conclusion and driving headfirst into another murder charge."

Satisfied with my answer, she turned her attention back to the scene in front of us.

At that moment, the girls and boys grouped together, and a discussion began. Dorian, Michael, and Calvin broke off, got into their car, and left. Kyle, Vanessa, and Jordan broke off after a few minutes and did the same, leaving Kayla and D-Wild by themselves, still in deep conversation. I was tempted to get out, but Kayla soon walked away from D-Wild toward the car. D-Wild got to his Magnum, and you could tell he was pissed because he peeled out, engine growling, and tires burning.

Getting into the car, Kayla remained silent for a second in deep thought. I let her have her moment, and then she began.

"Look, I know homegirl is your friend, but she's not part of the business we doing," Kayla said, measuring her words. "With that said, do you want to speak about this in front of her or wait until we finished and let her go bout her way?"

"I understand what she saying. If you want to drop me off, I'm okay with that. I appreciate you even picking me up."

Jazmine said seriously before I could respond. "She right that I'm not part of y'all business, but if you need me, you'll know where to find me."

"First off, if anything, you'll be dropping us off because this is your whip. Before you argue, the bill of sale and the title with your name on it is in the glove compartment." I informed her. "It's also a phone in there, too. I'm glad you said if I need you, I know where to find you. So, Kayla, to answer your question, I want her to know what she'll be getting into if I were to call on her in the clutch."

Kayla went on to explain the situation in full. Before the fire department made it, D-Wild found a note around the back of the club. Tasha, Ivy, DiVinci, and Capone set fire to my club, saying I could blame D-Wild and myself for it happening. For the disrespect from D-Wild over the years and me labeling Tasha and Ivy as snitches, they would terrorize our businesses and families until we were dead, everybody we loved suffered, and everything they loved burned to the ground. In other words, all-out war.

D-Wild had already gotten in touch with Papi and his own family and was en route to take care of the problem since he was brought in by name and the threat of his family. Dorian, Michael, and Calvin were going to get a few niggas and find out where DiVinci and Capone was located so they could cause some blood flow on their own. Kyle took Vanessa and Jordan out to Orange Mound since they weren't known so they could get information of their own to counter the damage done to Diamond House. Kayla was instructed to stay by my side and make sure I had some backup at all times since she was already riding with me. She said she planned to do that, plus more.

I, on the other hand, had other plans. I made a phone call to D-Wild's Uncle Leroy, letting him know that I was on the way to get the Lexus. My second call was to Cat Daddy, asking if he could meet me at a place of his choosing. He asked me where I was, and when I told him what I was about to do, he said the halfway point from where he was at the moment was South 3rd and Raines and to call when I got there.

By that point, Jazmine had the phone out of the glove compartment and was making a phone call of her own. Whoever was on the other end, she informed them that she was out but had to take care of a little business before she would be there. As an afterthought, she asked about two names, asked for their numbers, and hung up.

Pulling into the car lot, D-Wild's uncle had the Lexus in a parking spot but was nowhere in sight. As if seeing me, he came out of the building with keys in his hand, which was really only a key fob since the Lexus was a push button.

"Kayla, you driving the Lexus," I told her.

Kayla got out of the car as a response and made her way to D-Wild's uncle. They exchanged a few words, and he handed her the key chain. I waved a greeting, and he responded in turn. I waited for Kayla to have the car started and ready to go before we made our exit, two cars deep. My mind had already fast-forwarded to the conversation I was prepared to have with Cat Daddy and his brothers about my problem.

I must have been completely zoned because Jazmine was snapping her fingers in my face, trying to get my attention.

"My bad. What's up, girl?" I said, snapping back.

"I said I got some girls that are itching to put in some work." Jazmine started, rubbing her hands together. "They making sure they get they hands on a few guns for me since you say they supposed to be on that level."

"I'll let you know if we need them or not," I responded simply. "If this meeting goes like it's supposed to, then nobody else will be needed."

Ten minutes later, we were making a left from Raines onto South 3rd. One block over was a corner store leading into the neighborhood behind it. I called Cat Daddy and let him know where I was. He said he was on the way, letting me know he was right down the street.

When Kayla pulled in, she got out of the car and went into the store. While we were there, I decided to give Jazmine her second surprise while we waited. Reaching into my purse, I grabbed the check I had wrote out for fifteen hundred dollars and handed it to her.

"Girl, I'm not taking this!" she said, eyes wide. "You doing too much now!"

"If you don't stop arguing," I began reaching into my purse, pulling out my previous .380. "You gon' make me shoot you 'cause you offending me."

"I done had guns pulled on me to take my money," she said, sticking the check into her pocket with a smile. "Never to give me none, though. First time for everything, I guess."

Before I could say anything, a 95-96 money green Chevy

Caprice on what looked to be 22" Asanti rims pulled into the parking lot of the corner store. Knowing who it was, I told Jazmine to sit tight as I got out. You could hear and feel the music pumping from the Caprice. Mystikal's "Man Right Here (Here I go!)" gave them a grand entrance 'cause I was looking for them, and as Mystikal said, "Here I go! The man right chere!" I could only smile at the irony of it.

As soon as the car parked, Sir Brit got out the backseat and rushed inside the store without a word. Money Mike got out with a more practiced ease. He was wearing all white from head to toe. From his fedora to his wing tips, the man was fresh as fuck. His jewelry game was better than the average pimp's.

"Envy, looking good, baby girl," Money Mike said by way of greeting. "You a sight for sore eyes. I wish my hoes were more like you. Then I wouldn't have to train them so hard."

"You wouldn't have to train them 'cause they wouldn't be with you, big bro," Sir Brit from beside me. I never noticed him come out of the store. "When you put somebody like Envy in the mix, she gon' take all your money, take all your hoes, and end up training you. What's money, Envy?"

Sir Brit, the youngest but on the level with his brothers, had on all brown from his Kangol hat to his snake skins. He wasn't as refined as Money Mike but showed a swag and style that fit him to the T.

"You two niggas is crazy!" I said, reaching out for a hug to Sir Brit. "You get a hug first because you always know what a Boss Bitch can do."

"If I wasn't so secure with myself, I would take that as an

insult, Envy." Money Mike said, smiling. "I might even have to cancel your Playa's Ball membership."

"Now, Money," Cat Daddy's voice was heard as he finally got out of the Caprice and closed the door. "I'm glad that would be against rules and regulations. Then, I would have to revoke my membership. Without the Boss Bitch herself to attend the festivities, the Playa's Ball would be missing the top talent of the female category."

"Damn, gangsta! You feeling alright?!" I said when Cat Daddy made it around the Caprice. "Damn near ain't recognize you!"

Cat Daddy, who was usually best dressed, chose to dress down that day. His jewelry game was stiff, though. He wore an ice-white T-shirt, a pair of blue jeans, and a pair of Timberlands.

"The only thing on me under a hundred dollars is the draws and socks, baby," he said with flair. "Shirt by Canali 200, jeans by Salvatore Ferragamo 490, tank top underneath shirt by Boss 149, and shoes by Timberland 190. You can't help but recognize money when it's in front of you, Envy. You ought to be ashamed of yourself."

"I apologize, pimp. Let me get a hug to bring me back to my senses." I said mockingly, moving to give him a hug. "You know I see money, know money, and get money, but you went against your normal standards."

"You know, I'm wearing all this white, but I'm feeling like a black sheep," Money Mike said as I hugged Cat Daddy. "I'm the only one without the privilege of receiving one of your sisterly embraces, and I'm becoming self-conscious."

"That's a thought to be ignored," I commented, smiling, before continuing, "You damn well I'm gon' give you some love, pimpin. The young are always first, the suave one is next, and the last but not least is the mannish one."

Kayla chose that moment to come out of the store with a bag in her hand. When she caught sight of us four standing there and me hugging Money Mike, she came to a complete stop.

"Kayla, come here so I can introduce you," I said, trying to snap her out of that stunned silence.

"I know all three of them pimp ass niggas," she said, coming forward. "They all done shot they best shit trying to recruit a bitch to they hustle."

"Really, y'all?" I said with a laugh. "Y'all try to get my bitch to ride with y'all?"

"I'll answer for all three of us," Cat Daddy said with a wave. "We guilty as charged, but looking at her, you can't truly blame us."

"Amen!" Sir Brit agreed. "It wasn't so much as to try to pimp her out on my part completely. I just had to get a conversation with the gangsta that shot down my brothers. I damn near fell in love."

"You wouldn't know love if it hit you in the nuts and face with brass knuckles!" Money Mike said, making fun of Sir Brit. "He got a point, though. She declined Cat Daddy! I had to step into her presence and encounter the woman, yeah, I said it, the woman that had a strong enough mind to resist him at his top-level game."

"I lost three hundred dollars making a small wager that

I could at least get her number," Cat Daddy remarked with a smile.

The whole time they talked, Kayla had to smile at how honest they were in front of her.

"Who in the car?" Sir Brit asked, looking over my shoulder.

"That's my homegirl Jazmine. We just picked her up from jail a while ago," I answered. "No, she not that type of girl to end all questions."

I tapped the window, motioning Jazmine to get out since she was the cause of curiosity.

"What's up, bitch?" she said over the roof of the Audi.

"I want you to meet some friends of mine, and yes, they pimps. Among other things as well," I responded. "Cat Daddy, Money Mike, Sir Brit, meet Jazmine, and Jazmine, meet Cat Daddy, Money Mike, and Sir Brit."

As I said their names, each one raised their hand in a respective wave to acknowledge Jazmine.

"Nice to meet y'all," Jazmine responded with a wave and smile.

"She with you on this?" Cat Daddy asked out loud for her to hear.

"Yeah," I said simply. "Come around here, Jazmine."

"Alright, now that we got the greetings and the fun stuff out the way," Cat Daddy remarked as Jazmine stood beside me. "What's really good, Envy?"

Explaining myself, you could see all three brothers' faces lose all warmth that was in them and was replaced with an arctic freeze.

I was on Beale Street when I met these three. I was coming out of a club when this pimp nigga got in my personal space, trying to mack with his best game. I immediately went on alert and listened to him spit line after line of his weak game. When he was finished, I gave him a respectable "I'm not interested." Dude wasn't going for it, but instead of making a scene, I gave him a speech.

"One, the game, the hustle, and life are one and the same. They are 90% mental and 10% physical. Your game and hustle ain't even at 50% with that bubble gum machine ass mack you spitting. Two, your money ain't even long enough to approach me and hold my attention by the way you dressed. I'm a Boss Bitch, not a false bitch! Three, if you touch me again, I'm gon' put something so hot in your ass that by the time you cool off, you gon' look like a fried egg sunny side up!"

My hand was already in my purse, holding onto my pistol when he raised his hand, and I was about to pull the trigger when a voice brought pimp to a dead stop.

"Now, Pretty Ricky, if you so much as bring your hand a piece of an inch, you ain't gon' have to worry about her at all. That's a promise, a guarantee, and a short-order threat, pimp. She denied your advances, so advance your ass on down the road before you advance on a one-way ticket to four bullets sending you on your last journey."

Without a word or backward glance, Pretty Ricky took off at a brisk walk. I turned to acknowledge who made the statement only to see three fashionably dressed niggas who gave pimping a beauty mark. Seeing as they were pimps, obviously, I figured they wanted to be compensated.

"I ain't need no help with that pussy boy, and I hope y'all don't think I owe y'all anything because of it. If you are, I'd hate to disappoint y'all the way I did him."

Cat Daddy gave me a smile, saying, "Ma, we was compensated enough when you gave us a show of your standing. If anything, you got the approval that you are a Boss Bitch of status and breed. To show our sincerity, let us teach you game and sharpen game you already have. As you said, Life Hustle and Game are 90% mental and 10% physical. Ain't no ulterior motives coming from either one of us. Ask about us by name. Cat Daddy, Money Mike, and Sir Brit."

That was two years ago with a bunch of education.

When I finished giving them the details on everything as a whole, Money Mike was the first to respond to it. Cat Daddy remained quiet with fire in his eyes.

"Envy, you know we fuck with you the long way," Money said, removing his fedora, revealing a taper fade with perfect 360 waves like a honeycomb hideout. "So I ain't got to say much about what I'm willing to do."

"I'm with Money at one thousand percent. What do you want done bout it?" Sir Brit responded in agreement.

"Perfect deniability," Cat Daddy said in answer.

"What?" Money Mike and Sir Brit asked in unison.

"She wants perfect deniability," Cat Daddy repeated to them. "Orange Mound Money Gang and two hoes."

Money Mike and Sir Brit caught on and peeped at each other with devious smiles.

"Special request?" Cat Daddy asked.

"Bring me the two hoes," I answered after a thought. "Got something special for them."

No words were left as they moved to get back into their car and leave. So me, Jazmine, and Kayla followed suit.

CHAPTER NINE

O ver the next few days, because Diamond House was out of pocket, the girls that wasn't part of the Diamond Escorts all left to other clubs with my blessing. They all promised to come back when I was back up and running, however long it took. My attitude was as hot as the 90+ degrees we had been experiencing with the weather. I took a hit financially with the club up in smoke. So, Platinum Services office was the temporary headquarters for all business dealings, legal and illegal.

The days after losing some of my girls, I found out that the damage to Diamond House was so unrepairable that I would have to rebuild from the ground up all over again. That would cost me 30+ grand. So, I was in such a fucked-up mood that nobody gave me the news that I ended up getting when I popped up at The Red Carpet Hair Salon.

The salon was located in Orange Mound and had been since opening. Being that Kyle put Jordan over the spot, I had no reason to do pick-ups or payrolls. So, I decided to go get my hair done and talk shop with the girls when I got the shock of my life.

The Red Carpet was burnt out and abandoned, and the sign was hanging crooked. I didn't even stop. All I did was think of Rihanna singing, "Mama, Mama, Mama, I just shot a man down/in Central Station, in front of a big ol crowd" as I sped home, saying, "fuck the speed limit."

Making the left off Winchester onto Toholahoma, I ran the red, going sixty in the turning lane. I made the hard right into the shopping center with the Platinum Services office and made a beeline straight through the parking lot. Coming to a screeching tire-burning stop, I jumped out of my rented Camaro and headed right to the door. Who was there to meet me but the one I came to chew out?

"Where the fuck is Kyle?" I asked menacingly. "Don't tell me he's not here either 'cause his bike is outside."

One look at my face had Dorian pointing towards the back office, directing me away from him.

"Don't go anywhere," I instructed Dorian quietly. "I want you next."

Kyle picked that moment to come out of the back office with his phone to his ear in conversation with a scowl on his face. He looked up to see me, and the scowl deepened even further.

"I'll call you back," he said, ending the call. "Envy, we need to talk."

"You damn right, we need to talk! Let's talk about you not informing me that Red Carpet got burned up, and I had to just find out 'cause I wanted my hair done!" I began heatedly, building steam. "I want a mothafuckin' explanation with good enough reason for me not to get on you like a lion on a zebra's ass!"

"Let me give you your explanation first," he responded, equally heated. "As your business manager, I'm taking care of it. As the mothafucka responsible, I'm taking care of it. As your business manager, the mothafucka responsible, your second, and a very pissed off mothafucka, I'm taking fucking care of it!"

I had never seen Kyle with as so much as a little attitude that his outburst took me by total surprise.

"Second, Jordan was there when it went down, and she got hit with the brick that crashed through the window before the bottled cocktail came in and set the bitch on fire." Kyle continued with enough heat to singe my eyebrows. "So, Kyle is on the back burner, and King Kai is taking care of it. I called in some help from the H. That's who I was on the phone with, 'cause they at the airport now waiting for me to pick them up. Jordan's okay. She just needed stitches in the back of her head. So, if you'll excuse me, I'm bout to turn this city red."

Before I could answer, Kyle walked past me and out the door. He didn't get on his motorcycle, though. He got into Dorian's car, an old-school Monte Carlo, and took off.

"How long you knew about this?" I turned to Dorian, asking.

"About an hour and a half ago," Dorian answered, taking a seat in one of the chairs in front of a window. "I asked him the same question you did. Want to know what he told me?"

"What?" I responded.

"He felt responsible for Jordan 'cause he brought her there with the rest of them. You didn't know all four of them stayed together?" With a shocked look for my answer, he continued. "He also said he knew we would try to stop him from doing what he needed to do, and he wasn't gon' lay right."

"He's right. I wouldn't let him," I remarked.

"Me either, but only because we know the city and he doesn't. Plus, he ain't been in the streets since he got in with you." Dorian said with a pointed look. "I wanted him to ride with Michael, Calvin, and me, but we all know how you would act. He gave us his history and resume as King Kai, but you only knew the business side named Kyle. My advice, believing he kept it to himself to take care of himself, take it easy on him and let him ride."

After listening to Dorian, I knew he was right. I've known Dorian and them longer than I've known Kyle, so I could see where he was coming from when he said to let Kyle do his thing. Then I thought back to a conversation with D-Wild I had a while back. He told me as much when he explained about the Suit and Tie/Street nigga. So, my decision was made.

While everybody was on their gangsta shit, I was walking 'round like the problem would solve itself and not thinking like a Gangsta Boss Bitch. I had to put the Boss Bitch on standby and go Gangsta mode.

I stood there, thinking on what Kyle and Dorian said as

a whole, and had an idea.

"Dorian," I said, getting his attention. "I want you, Michael, Calvin, Kayla, and Vanessa at my house in three hours. When Kyle gets back, you tell him to come, too, and bring his friends with him. I got other calls to make."

He immediately pulled out his phone, and I headed for the door with my phone in hand, preparing to make my calls. Thinking on D-Wild and Dorian's words and Kyle's, it was time to get my head out of the sand and bring heat to the situation.

****

After shopping at the liquor store to grab a few bottles and a couple bags of ice, I sat waiting for everybody to arrive. My phone calls went out to D-Wild, Cat Daddy, and Jazmine, and they agreed to show up. I had to give my address to Jazmine and Cat Daddy. Them not having my address didn't mean I didn't trust them. Every time I dealt with Cat Daddy, he always wanted to meet up on the move. Jazmine just got out, and she was getting her shit together, but we stayed connected over the phone.

Another hour had passed, and everybody was there. Cat Daddy and his brother, D-Wild and Al, Dorian, Michael and Calvin, Kayla, Vanessa, and Jordan, plus Kyle and his group.

I had to make the introductions since nobody knew Cat Daddy, Money Mike, and Sir Brit by face, and Kyle made his intros. His friends, part of a clique called Kingsgate Gang out of Southwest Houston, were named King Ross and King

Polo, respectively. We were still waiting on Jazmine.

"Listen, the only reason I asked everybody to come here to meet is because we all got the same objective, but we endangering the goal by not knowing who your ally is if you were to run into them." I began, not wanting to wait on Jazmine any longer. "Now, Cat Daddy, Money Mike, and Sir Brit only tie to this through me, like A1 with D-Wild and King Ross and King Polo with King Kai. Right now, we've allied but not fully committed to affiliating with each other as a whole. A common goal brought us together."

The solid knock on the front door drew everybody's attention, cutting me off from my train of thought. Without a second thought, I went to my purse on the kitchen counter and pulled out my .380.

"Who is it?!" I asked loudly, making it to the door.

"Jazmine," the muffled response came back.

The tension that built up eased out of my shoulders as I opened the door.

"Hey, girl. Sorry, I'm late," Jazmine said with three chicks behind her.

"What's up, girl? Don't worry about it. Come in," I said, stepping to the side.

When she didn't move, I looked at her face and saw the wide-eyed expression from her and her friends, making me looking back.

Every nigga, excluding the girls, had a pistol in their hands and was facing the door without so much as a sound being made.

"It's cool," I said, motioning for them to chill.

"Damn, bitch! What you packing for in your own house?" Jazmine asked, probably after she noticed I also had a pistol in my hand.

"If you was anybody else, short of God himself, it was gon' be a problem," I answered, turning back to let them in.

"It's 3:00 pm. It could've been Jehovah's Witnesses at the door," Jazmine stated.

"Well, Jehovah was gon' witness them get an early departure to the afterlife and meet them at the pearly gates, apologizing for not sending a sign not to come to my house right now while we all were here," I said, closing the door as the last chick came in.

Jazmine went into a laughing fit, bringing nervous chuckles out of her friends.

"I was explaining to everybody about who's affiliated with me and who are allies due to one person or the other," I explained as we reached the living room. "Don't want to run into somebody and get the wrong idea 'cause we see somebody somewhere. Since everybody doing their own thing with their own crew of people, I wanted everybody to know who not to hurt in the process of they mission."

I made the introduction of Jazmine to everybody and let her introduce her friends. They were part of her Summer's Ave crew called B.A.D. Bitches. Business and Destruction was what B.A.D. stood for. The first girl's name was Egypt, the second was Porsche, and the third was Kash.

It was Kash that gave me pause. She looked so out of place that you would think she was a sheep in a den of wolves. Cat Daddy must have felt the same way because his next move and statements brought us entertainment.

"Check it out, ma. You look like you ready to crawl into a corner and start crying in a minute," Cat Daddy said, testing the girl. "Now, if the pistols scared you into silence, I know something that'll bring life back to you."

Kash looked at Jazmine, who stood blank-faced cause she already met Cat Daddy and seen I didn't stop him. When Kash saw Jazmine remain silent, her attention went to Cat Daddy.

"What's your name?" Kash asked.

"Cat Daddy," he responded, waiting to see how she responded.

"Well, Cat Daddy, I didn't know what kind of party this was, so the pistols shocked me a little bit," she said, transforming before our eyes. "As for crawling and hiding or crying, wrong bitch. Now, if what you got in mind to bring me life got to do with your dick, I suggest you keep it to yourself, or you can rest assured that before the night over with, pistol or not, I'll have you sucking your own dick."

Silence took over the room, and Cat Daddy's stone-faced expression changed to a smile.

"If I was serious, that statement would have had you being fed in the clouds, but on second thought, it was an answer similar to that, which is the reason I fuck with Envy," Cat Daddy explained, then looked at me. "I heard of this chick's crew but never seen them before. They put in a lot of work in North Memphis, as they said, with Business and Destruction. Whichever come first."

When I didn't answer, he looked back at Kash.

"Now, for you," he said, getting up and making his way across the room to stand in front of Kash. "Let me apologize to you. I didn't mean to offend you, but I had to see where y'all mind was at, and by you looking the most innocent, plus being introduced last, I had to test your crew through you. No hard feelings.?"

When he reached his hand out, Kash didn't hesitate to shake his hand.

"Oh yeah," he said with a smile. "Envy can tell you that if I was trying to do anything with you, my game would be tighter, and I would be a respectable gentleman. Not a lame trying to downgrade in the least."

"I would hope not," Kash remarked. "Then I would be disappointed to finally meet the man with the name and rep you have, only to meet a watered-down wannabe."

Money Mike and Sir Brit couldn't seem to hold it any longer and erupted in rambunctious laughter, causing Cat Daddy to smile.

"I think I just fell in love," Cat Daddy said, still smiling, hand over his heart.

Kash's response was to smile and walk away.

This caused more laughter from Money Mike and Sir Brit.

The clowning went on for a few minutes, with the girls greeting everybody and finding somewhere to sit. That was how I realized that I needed to keep the people in this room on my team even after this was done.

It was D-Wild that brought us back to being serious. I did my part by getting everybody involved in one room, and the rest was up to them. So, D-Wild choosing to speak up gave me a chance to evaluate how everyone regarded each other.

As everyone explained what it was they were contributing to the situation, they were listened to respectfully and asked questions. Each group offered their services to the others, saying that to keep things under wraps, this should be the only group involved. So far, it was Cat Daddy who made the most progress looking for DiVinci, Capone, Tasha, and Ivy. Though their clique was based in Orange Mound, Capone and DiVinci moved out the hood and was floating somewhere in South Memphis. They were constantly moving but sending orders back to their crew to fuck with my shit. That was when D-Wild informed me that he took a hit at two barbershops that M.A.C. Mafia owned and separated.

"Hold up," Cat Daddy said to D-Wild. "When Envy said your name was D-Wild, I let it pass 'cause I know how niggas like to copycat other real niggas names. Now, you say M.A.C. Mafia, so I know you legit. After this, I need to get your undivided attention alone, if you don't mind."

"Whatever you got to say, you can say it now," D-Wild remarked not too happily. "I ain't got shit to hide from nobody here."

"You sure?" Cat Daddy responded calmly. When he didn't get a change in answer, he continued. "You used to work for Papi, if I'm not mistaken."

"What Papi got to do with this?!" I asked in confusion.

"Your dad?" Cat Daddy asked, shocked, then looked at Money Mike and Sir Brit.

"Yeah, Papi, her dad, and I used to work for him,"

D-Wild said, tensing up. "Envy is my baby too, so what of it, my guy?"

"First and foremost, calm down. If it was heat coming your way, it wouldn't be a damn thing you could do to stop it," Cat Daddy assured calmly. "I used to do odd jobs for Papi back when he was still in the game. He never mentioned a daughter, though. To ease your minds so I can explain myself, hold on. Money, call Papi."

Money Mike did as was told, and a second later, there was a ringing over the speakerphone.

"Money Mike," Papi answered, his voice unmistakable. "What do I owe the pleasure of your call?"

"That would be me, Papi. It's Cat Daddy," Cat Daddy responded.

"Ahhh! What can I do for you?" Papi asked.

"Well, I'm sitting here with D-Wild and your daughter Envy, you never told me about," Cat Daddy answered, looking straight into my eyes.

"Please don't tell me there is a hit out on either one of their heads," Papi asked worriedly. "I'll double the pay, whatever it is."

"Papi, you worry too much," Cat Daddy said with a smile. "I'm actually working with them both with Envy's problem."

"Oh," Papi said simply. "Why call me then?"

"I wanted them to hear your voice to verify my next words to them," Cat Daddy explained, still staring at me in the eye. "They can hear you if you got something to say, and yes, Money Mike and Sir Brit are with me."

"I'd hate to be whoever you going after," Papi commented.

"Anyway, Envy and D-Wild, listen carefully to me. I don't know how you encountered Cat Daddy and his brothers, but you did a very good job in doing so. You do good to keep them close. They are like a heat-insulated coat in -9 degree weather when it comes to problem-solving, and they may be able to teach a few things to you both in any category, sophisticatedly and professionally. They are not much older than you, Envy, but they are beyond your years. Hell, I taught D-Wild, but I think they even surpass what I taught him. With that said, I can rest easy knowing you got D-Wild and the band of brothers watching over you."

The line went dead, and Money Mike put the phone in his pocket.

The room remained silent as me and D-Wild stared at each other in disbelief at what was just done. If these niggas used to run for Papi, that meant they so far deep in the game, then what I had seen over the years didn't even scratch the surface of what they were capable of.

"Now," Cat Daddy said, bringing us back. "Papi was the only one person we've ever thrown all our cards in within affiliation."

"The old man been fucking with us since before we got our rep," Money Mike spoke up. "He stayed coming to Graceland where we was putting our game down, and we stayed soaking game and putting in work."

"After he seen we was relentless and wouldn't be denied our part in the hustler's game, he asked a simple question," Cat Daddy said, stepping in. "'What's your hustle?' Knowing the answer would change everything, and I answered, speaking for all of us, saying money."

"We were all going by different names then and knew we needed something that could be used in all our hustle areas," Money Mike explained. "We built our names after we decided to enter pimpin' into our hustle."

"Papi kept us going, using us for dope runs other niggas was scared to make," Cat Daddy said, leaning back. "We'd make the runs and pop our pistols if it was problems."

"When I decided I was fully committed, Cat Daddy and Money Mike took off, taking me with them," Sir Brit finally broke in. "We took every fighting class we could find and found places that wasn't scared to let three young niggas learn the art of firearms."

"We disappeared for a minute and came back broke, but we had skills that we learned coming up," Cat Daddy took the lead. "Papi caught up with us and we explained what we went to do. You know what Papi said?"

"If you want a job, I'll put you to work right now," Money Mike said. "Of course, we said yeah."

"He pointed at a nigga and said dude owed him some money and been holding out," Cat Daddy explained, continuing the tale all the way through. "He said he wanted him dealt with, but he wanted it done in such a fashion that we got away clean, and he never got implicated. Dude was a broke-down pimp, but a pimp, so we used his ego against him right then and there to soak up his game for our purpose. Two days later, they found dude butt naked with a note taped to his forehead."

"Pay your debts or end in death," D-Wild finished for

him. "That was y'all? They still ain't find his tongue, dick, and balls."

"Safe to say, nobody never knew, and we worked for Papi exclusively until he retired, but we told him that he always got us if he need us," Cat Daddy concluded.

"But he never told you about me?" I asked, gaining an understanding of the situation.

"I understand completely," Cat Daddy responded. "We was hustling, pimpin, and knocking niggas off left and right. We got bold and put our calling card out there, and got our names known from North Memphis to across state line, from East Memphis to West Memphis, Arkansas. Your pops knew all this, plus nobody knew we worked for him, and we only recently found out he had a wife after he retired. You, on the other hand, weren't known about until today."

"So, in other words, Envy, you got a squad," Money Mike informed. "We already fucked with you 'cause you earned our respect. That's why Cat Daddy made the decision to school you in whatever you wanted to know."

"But now," Cat Daddy said with a serious face. "We know about Papi, so we gon' make sure to move heaven and earth to bring hell to this problem you got."

"D-Wild," Sir Brit said, getting his attention. "He was likely gon' tell you that same deal about you being part of Papi, but knowing now that you with Envy, too, the same goes for you."

"And anybody that ride with you from here on out," Money Mike said. "But our loyalty rides solely with you, Envy, and only you. D-Wild got support, but you got the equivalent of the whole U.S. military behind you now. D-Wild, I know you a Marine, so don't take offense to that statement.

"My guy, now that we got that piece of info out the way, we can rock this bitch on out," D-Wild responded with a genuine smile that reached his eyes. "Envy, seeing as nobody has any objections."

He paused and looked around the room. When nobody said anything, he finished his statement.

"What you want to do?" D-Wild asked, taking a sip of his drink.

"Okay," I said with newfound confidence. "This what I need from each of you..."

CHAPTER TEN

S itting in my 745, a massive amount of considerable thoughts ran through my mind as Neyo's "Champagne Life" blasted from the speakers. He spoke to me in volumes about the lifestyle I was living. He said, "Your troubles are only a bubble in a champagne glass."

Two burnt-up businesses fucked up my income. Still, I hadn't lost sight of the biggest picture. My set goal was to retire, own a big enough stock and real estate, and invest, and all I had to do was get electronic updates every time money was added to my account. So, it really upset me that my money was being cut by more than half with these damages done.

Making the right on Shelby Drive from Millbranch, I was leaving Da Haven from having a sit down with Dorian's brother and head of the Blackhaven Gorillas, Magic. With me knowing people from different crews but not having my own, I needed to see if there were chicks around that wasn't part of his outfit that I could recruit for my service. Yeah, I got Cat Daddy and his brothers on call, but that was for the male problems I had, and I needed females.

Jazmine was down with me and brought her B.A.D. Bitches with her, but they had their own business and crew built with Jazmine at the head of the table. D-Wild advised me that I had Kayla, Vanessa, and Jordan to start with, and he had a point. I even told them I needed some more thorough bitches to add on with us. They asked if we had a name, and I told them I'd get back to them on that subject.

Cruising with my head focused on my next moves like I was studying a chess board, my thoughts were as clear as the blue sky I was passing under. Everything went back to the beginning of this whole situation.

Snitching.

I understood once I could figure out what led these two crumb ass hoes to go against the code of every hood in every nation around the world, then I could better grasp the circumstances so I could ease my curiosity. Plus, I could better deal with the situation on where those hoes got the nuts to go against the grain. That was why I wanted them two tramps alive cause it goes deeper than the surface shows. If I was a simple-minded bitch, instead of a woman with deep knowledge and ability to think, I would believe they were the brains to it all. Too bad I knew those hoes don't think anything through. 'Cause if they had brains, they wouldn't go for my businesses. They would come for me harder than snitching and burning buildings.

TI's "Stand Up" suddenly came through my speakers,

and it took me a second to remember that I had my phone's Bluetooth to my stereo system.

"Hello?" I answered, trying to remember who I set the ringtone for.

"Got some info for you that you might want," Cat Daddy's voice crooned over the speakers. "You want it now or later?"

Oh yeah, Cat Daddy was TI, Money Mike was Trick Daddy, and Sir Brit was Lil Wayne. Very fitting when it came to their characters and individual personalities.

"You can give me the info now while I'm driving in case I get an idea and want to move on it," I responded, slowing down the car to 5mph, under the speed limit. "So, give it to me straight shot, no chaser."

"We pinpointed the two niggas and two bitches," he revealed with something in his voice. "They been right under our noses the whole fucking time, and I don't like chasing my tail getting outfoxed by some rudimentary ass niggas."

He went on to explain that they had remained in Orange Mound but was telling people that they were in different areas of the city so word wouldn't get out that they never left. They actually slipped up and was seen in a strip club on the same block as my salon. Tasha and Ivy wasn't with DiVinci and Capone. But when they left the club that Cat Daddy and his brothers so happened to be at, they followed them back to a spot and had been sitting on it all night trying to gain the routine. It was a few niggas in and out, and they even spotted the two hoes coming out, chopping it up with niggas like they were royalty. The spot was actually the main spot for Orange Mound Money Gang meetings and business dealings.

"Y'all still got eyes on them?" I asked with a destination in mind.

"Yeah. What you want done?" Cat Daddy answered, letting me know that the next move was mine.

"I want to let Kyle bomb on them niggas, but I want them hoes," I responded, trying to figure out a way to kill two birds with one stone. "Can you coordinate with him and his homeboys so both can get done?"

"Sure," he answered simply.

"Where do you want them to meet with you?" I asked.

"How bout you give me the number so I can call him?" he guided easily. "Perfect deniability, remember? At least til you get the two renegade ass hoes in your clutches anyway."

I gave him the number and asked him to take care of Kyle and keep him as safe as possible without jeopardizing his health.

After making calls to everyone else to let them know that they could stop their searches and go along as if there was no problem, I decided to go talk to Papi. There were still times that I asked for his advice without giving him the details or even an idea of what I had going on. Though he knew I had Cat Daddy and his brothers in my company, as well as D-Wild, it was perfect deniability for him if ever asked.

It took me fifteen minutes to reach the house. With Momma's car gone, it was obvious that Papi was home by himself. When Queen came from the side of the house at a dead run, I knew Papi had to be in the backyard, most likely in his shed, with Queen as the bodyguard with a free roam of the yard. So, I just parked in front of the yard as Queen watched, alert. When I got out, she barked, her tail wagging happily.

"Hey, girl!" I greeted her with love and scratch behind the ear. "Where's Papi?"

She immediately headed toward the backyard in front of me, knowing I'd follow her. Walking behind her, I tried to figure out how to phrase the words for the conversation I wanted to have with Papi.

When I rounded the corner, instead of heading to his shed, Queen turned towards the backdoor. Papi was sitting at the handmade, long picnic table with two other men I initially didn't recognize.

"Uncle E! Miguel!" I shouted excitedly. "Papi didn't tell me y'all were here!"

Uncle B, Mr. Enrique Santiago, was Papi's older brother. At 5'9" with a stocky frame and still jet-black hair slicked back, you would think he was younger. He had his old school swag going with the red and white Nike jumpsuit, red and white Nike Cortez, and red Kangol cap. He wore a simple gold chain, watch, bracelet, and rings adorning his wedding and right pinky fingers.

"How's my niece?" Uncle E greeted me, giving me a hug. "I hear you got hit by the policia, but got out. What you into?"

"Since you ask so nicely," I stated mockingly with a smile. "I'll get to that after I get a hug from Miguel."

"I thought you were going to act funny with me, and I was really gonna be upset," Miguel said, opening his arms.

"Not my favorite cousin!" I responded, moving in for the

hug. Miguel was Uncle E's son and spitting image. Miguel, also known as Gunz to those in the lifestyle, had a reputation for keeping a variety of pistols and automatic rifles and wasn't hesitant on busting that hot lead either. He was older than me by two years but carried himself like an old-school veteran in the game. His attire told you he was bout his business but would turn up if need be. Wearing an egg-white colored blazer over an ice-white tee tucked into his white pants and leading to a pair of white low-top sneakers, you would think he wasn't bout that life. Damned fool you'd be.

When I gave him a hug, I shouldn't have been surprised to feel the guns under his arms. I opened the jacket only to reveal him wearing shoulder holsters with shining chrome pieces tucked into them. I just gave him a look and closed his jacket back.

"Did I interrupt something?" I asked suspiciously, looking from Miguel to Papi.

"Why don't you take a seat, Envy," Papi suggested, motioning me to sit beside him.

****

Pulling away from the house, I never thought I would feel so clear-minded. The conversation I just left was along the lines that if things got to be more than I could handle, I could call family. 'Cause whether I knew it or not, all I had to do was call Miguel, and he would make it disappear. I kindly explained that everything was under control after I gave them the recap on all that had happened. I didn't say who all was involved or their parts in it, but I did assure them that I had enough backup. I didn't turn down the free advice given, though.

Just like steel sharpens steel, listening to advice from an experienced mind with an overflowing vault of knowledge, you have no choice but to become like the mind that teaches you.

Uncle E told me that he understood I was making a name for myself and was succeeding. The only thing was that I didn't have to hide who I was and what I did from family. I could come out of the shadows and show my position of power. Regardless of whether I knew it or not, I had more backup with my family because I was born into something bigger than me. Though Papi retired, he still held a seat at the table with the family organization.

I had my own thing, though. I was still building my team and business. Everything I did and achieved was done outside of family business. I didn't want people saying that they only did this or that or respected me only because I was Papi's daughter. I wasn't having that. I let it be known that I would keep everything in mind for future reference, but I wanted to take care of things on my own.

TI's "Stand Up" boomed through the speakers, and this time, I didn't hesitate to reach my phone to answer.

"Yes?" I answered, wanting good news.

"Christmas is early this year," Cat Daddy spoke, letting me know things were done. "You want your presents?"

"Where do I have to pick them up?" I asked blankly, not wanting to expose my excitement.

"We over in your neck of the woods right now," he

answered, then continued, "You familiar with Knight Arnold and Tchoulahoma, where the auto shop is by the airport?"

"I'm on my way there right now," I responded, making a right on a street named Queensbridge that leads to Tchoulahoma. "Give me five minutes."

"Kyle and his goons got presents for you, too," Cat Daddy stated, shocking me.

"Now, that is a surprise," I responded. "D-Wild been contacted yet?"

"We all here. Wanted you to be the last to know so you could make an entrance," Cat Daddy answered with a chuckle. "That way, they can know who got their presents and enjoyed them."

"Three minutes," I said as I hit Tchoulahoma and made the left. "I hope the wrapping paper is beautiful."

"Baby girl, now you know that for a Boss Bitch, we go all out to accommodate your acquired taste and style," Cat Daddy said slyly. "You gon' love the way this has come together."

"Almost there," I voiced, then hung up the line.

So, they went and got them all and had them tied up, nice and tight, waiting for me. They must have really been slipping, or these niggas were that damn good. I wasn't gon' look a gift horse in the mouth. At least court could be run on all they asses at the same time, and I could get answers.

Pulling up to the auto shop, the gate was closed. I saw Dorian's Monte Carlo first, then Cat Daddy's Caprice. Kyle's Tahoe grabbed my attention because he hardly ever used it. Usually, he drove his Cadillac CTS around because the

Tahoe was for…

I had to smile for not catching it the first time. Kyle's side hustle was being a landscaper. So, that was how he got all of them hoes at once. Before I could think anymore on it, I honked my horn twice. After a minute, Kyle stepped out, came to the gate, opened it, and closed it behind me when I pulled in. I parked behind Kyle's Tahoe and got out. That was when I spotted A1's Eldorado and Vanessa's champagne-colored 2015 Nissan Altima on twenty-inch Asanti rims. The only car I didn't see as I went in was the Audi I gave to Jazmine.

"Jazmine not showing?" I asked Kyle curiously.

"Said she ain't want to be part of the end result but could always get at her if you need her," Kyle answered. "Envy, look, I need to apologize…"

I cut him off with a raise of my hand.

"You don't owe me no apology at all. I took my role too far, and you were right about your position. If I didn't trust you to handle things without me micromanaging you, I should not have gave you the status, but I do, and I did." I gave him a smile before I continued, "Besides, King Kai must have needed to rise from his slumber for this. If you were a weak nigga, I wouldn't have ever made you part of my business in any aspect. You got a right to defend this family's honor like everybody else. So, from now on, I'm cutting your leash. I still want my reports 'cause this is still my business, and I will always be critical of moves made within my business. Now, on the other hand, I won't question you or ask you to do what's not comfortable to you as a man. With that being said, let me get to these headaches of ours."

"Thank you, Envy," Kyle responded, leading me from the office to the garage where our guests were waiting.

As we entered, Kyle moved to the side, and I looked at four chairs with four people bound and gagged facing me. So, I made my entrance, slow and deliberate, watching as Tasha and Ivy's eyes locked onto me, and they started to fidget around. Kayla came over and rewarded them both with vicious slaps, causing their heads to snap to the side. The fear in their eyes as they looked back at me spoke volumes.

I looked at Capone and DiVinci, and I was disappointed. These niggas were actually quite handsome, but their defects were noticeable. The defects must have been inflicted by hand, but that was their own fault. They both had busted lips and black eyes, which were on their way to closing. Blood was all over their white t-shirts.

"Well, hello," I said, trying to get their attention. "I didn't expect to have all these people present at one time."

They both looked up. Their eyes burned with defiance at spotting me, showing they had a little heart left. That would change, though.

"Remove the gags from all of them, please," I requested. "To let y'all know, if you piss me off, I will make your deaths slow and painful. So cooperate, or I'll demonstrate."

As Dorian went to remove the gags, I pulled my .380 and set my purse on the floor. Before I could take a step, D-Wild stopped me, holding out a .25 with one hand and the other hand held out.

"If I'm right, that .380 is in your name. No evidence, no

trace, no case," he explains. "So, take this and give me that, or put it away."

I didn't reply as I put the .380 in my waist and took the .25 from him. I ejected the clip to check what I was working with, replaced it, and made sure it was one in the chamber. D-Wild smiled and stepped away off to the side to stand next to A1. Dorian had already removed the gags when I reached the guests of honor.

"The first thing I want to know is why did y'all fuck with me and my businesses, burning them down?" When nobody spoke, I quickly became frustrated. "Don't everybody answer at once."

When there was still silence, I looked around the room.

"Have they been this quiet since y'all got them?" I asked, annoyed.

There was a collective "yes" around the room.

"Okay," I said simply and shot either Capone or DiVinci in the shoulder, getting a scream out of him. "Which one are you?"

"That's DiVinci!" Capone said from the first chair.

"Oh, so you can speak," I remarked. "I thought we needed somebody who knew sign language or a translator."

"Envy, please, don't do this! Please!" Ivy spoke up.

"Bitch, what?!" I replied emphatically. "You shouldn't have done what you did, and we most likely wouldn't be here. You two bitches started off this chain of events by hating on a bitch and then snitching me out. Did you tell these niggas about that before you involved them in this affair of no return?"

From the look on Capone's face, they obviously hadn't. He confirmed it with his next statement.

"Say, ma, I don't know nothing bout no snitching shit. We don't rock like that. From our understanding, it was the other way around," Capone said, shocking me and causing me to look from him back to Tasha and Ivy.

The truth was apparent from the hang of their heads. I walked over closer to them with a look of bewilderment.

"So, you bitches snitched me out, then try to label me as the snitch when I'm the one who was facing a murder charge? Seriously?" I asked, getting hot under the collar. "You rat ass bitches got these niggas to ride with you 'cause they thought I was a rat."

I looked back at Capone and DiVinci and felt sorry for them, but they should have done their research, and I let them know it.

"See, that's the problem with tender dick niggas, and the reason I ask for a person's resume and credentials. I don't like weaknesses," I began, eyeing them disdainfully. "The weakness is the lack of research into these hoes' story. D-Wild, I told you what happened, but I know you also did your own research, am I right?" I stated. He confirmed, and I continued. "That's called making sure you ain't on the wrong side of the bullshit. Now, if you would have been rocking with these hoes for years, I could understand you just riding with no questions asked. Hell, I been knowing D-Wild damn near all my damn life, and he checked to make sure I was legit."

I switched the pistol to my left hand and punched Ivy

in the face. When I connected, I felt the crunch, letting me know her nose was broken as blood began to flow onto her shirt. I backhanded Tasha with the pistol, opening a gash on her cheek.

"See, I feel sorry for you two niggas only because you didn't know what you were getting into. My sympathy ends there for y'all cause, after that, you guilty as charged in my book." I informed them, watching them from in front of Tasha and Ivy.

"Ma, I'm telling you we didn't know these hoes was snakes, or we would have never fucked with them in any way," Capone said, pleading his case. "We don't rock like that. Let us make it, ma. We won't even bother about the shoulder shot on DiVinci. You got my word, on my set."

"I'm supposed to forget about burning my businesses down and the brick that hit one of my sisters and split her shit? That's what you asking me?" I asked. "I'm supposed to let you go, accept what happened, and believe you won't be a future problem for me or my business? That's what you saying?"

Capone remained silent, but it was DiVinci who responded through clenched teeth.

"Look, I understand your position to the fullest, and I would feel the same way. Shit, I wouldn't even entertain us or a conversation," DiVinci said, in pain. "I got a proposition for you if you willing to give it a thought."

I was looking at DiVinci with a newfound respect because even though he got a bullet in his shoulder, he was still showing heart.

"I'll hear your proposition with no promises 'cause I'm not the only one in this," I began. "I'll say this, I live on the three P's in my life. Pleasure, Power, and Profit, and you have to touch each one. From pleasure comes power, which ultimately leads to profit. So, go ahead."

DiVinci took a deep breath, clenched his jaw, then looked me in the eye before he started.

"First and foremost, I'll gladly put a bullet in these two hoes for getting us into this shit. Second, we'll happily reimburse you for the damages, even though we don't know the cost. We'll agree to work it off if you let us. Until then, we'll be in your debt and at your call, personally. Third, this bullet in my shoulder I deserve for my stupidity of not checking into what was really popping," DiVinci tried to roll his shoulder and hissed in pain but continued. "Lastly, I want to apologize to you and your family for our part in this. To be honest, even though M.A.C. Mafia don't know it, our beef been dead with them. So, don't think we got in this to get at y'all, D-Wild. We actually grew over the years and understood our error. We was young, trying to make names for ourselves, but we got under some vets and learned a few things about life and hoes. We just ain't know about these hoes at all."

"As for the actual vets, we had nothing to do with them, but we did offer them protection 'cause we was fucking them and the lies they told us," Capone finished off.

"Anybody got anything to say on what was said by DiVinci on his proposition?" I asked the room after a minute of silence.

Personally, I would take pleasure in holding power over them and making a profit. Though, it wouldn't be too much of a profit unless I added interest on the damages along with giving them their lives.

Kyle broke away from his group, as did D-Wild, Dorian, Kayla, and Cat Daddy, to stand on either side of me. That by itself gave me mixed answers on what was going to happen next.

I gained understanding when they remained silent. Whatever decision I made was up to me, and they would back me up on whatever it was. We all knew the futures of Tasha and Ivy were forfeited, but Capone and DiVinci were up for grabs. By Tasha and Ivy not denying anything said, we knew that they were telling the truth as best they knew.

"I'll tell you what," I began, my decision made. "Capone, you gon' get a bullet to match DiVinci. That's gon' be first." I said before I shot him in the shoulder. When he stopped screaming in agony, only breathing hard, I continued. "The damages are at a hundred grand plus 'cause I got to rebuild from the ground up. I don't know what kind of money you making, and I'm doubting that if I put a number out there, you could cover it. Since you willing to forget the bullet in your shoulder, is your partner willing to do the same? Right now, I don't believe I should trust either of you as far as I can throw you, and I don't even think I could lift one of you off the ground." I paused in effect. "You said you would gladly put a bullet in these hoes, which you might get a chance to do, but before we get to that..."

I turned my attention to Tasha and Ivy, who were staring

at me with pleading in their eyes. I automatically got pissed. They had the balls to come at me but wanted to tuck tail when it got gangsta. I walked up to Tasha and cocked my arm back, letting it rocket with full force, landing a solid blow on her jaw. Without missing a step, I backhanded Ivy with a closed hand, catching her flush in the mouth.

"Easy way or hard way," I said repeatedly. "You two bitches went against me because, why?"

When they only hung their heads, it infuriated me to no end.

"Gag 'em," I requested. "Anybody got a knife they don't want no more?"

Cat Daddy went into his pocket and pulled out a knife, flicked it open, and handed it to me handle first. Upon seeing the knife, Ivy came to life with a shout.

"Wait! Wait!" she screamed. "I'll tell you!"

Dorian looked at me, and I nodded, so he backed off but remained behind them.

"I hope what came out your mouth next is better than your head game," I stated.

"We was fucked up 'cause you cut us off the way you did, so we was hanging with some chick out of South Memphis. She said she was trying to expand and would let us run this part if we could get you out of the way. She even gave us the idea that if we had something on you, we could get you out the way without bloodshed," Ivy explained. "After we did it, we knew the shit wasn't cool, so we disappeared on the D.A. and wouldn't return his calls. That way, they ain't have no evidence on you without either or both of us testifying.

When you got out, we was trying to tell you, but you wasn't trying to hear a word we was saying."

"That's when we hooked up with these two dudes and gave them the story so they could ride with us. We had to sit tight before we gave it to them like we just got out," Tasha cut in. "Then we ran into you at the car wash, and your girl right there got in it. It was supposed to be between us, but she added to it. Then A1, yeah, we know him... he had to put us on blast. So, we went back and gave Capone and DiVinci the business on the snitching, the fight, and A1 getting in it. The end."

"You bitches played it like he put his hands on y'all!" DiVinci yelled. "Bitch, you got us in the middle of some fuck shit! When I meet you in hell, I'm gon' make a deal with Satan to personally torture you hoes for eternity!"

"Alright! Enough!" I said, gaining back control of the situation. "Who is this bitch out of South Memphis?"

When Tasha and Ivy eyed each other instead of answering, irritation took over. Before anybody knew what happened, my foot was planted into Tasha's chest, sending her and the chair backward. Before she landed, my left hand swung with everything I had, hitting Ivy in the side of the head and sending her and her chair sideways. Dorian went to lift Tasha back up when I stopped him.

"Leave them bitches right there! Obviously, they think this is a fucking game!" I shouted angrily, stepping around to stand over their heads. "This bitch right here think she extra smart!" I emphasized by kicking Ivy in the stomach. "Let me reassure you two bitches of something!"

I stepped to Tasha and stomped her in the stomach, leaving my foot planted as I bent down, putting the pistol to her head. She struggled to catch her breath as my weight bared down into her stomach.

"Now, if I have your attention, I believe I asked you a question on the identity of this mysterious person you were telling me about," I began calmly as I pressed the pistol into Tasha's forehead. "All the procrastination y'all doing ends here. So, we can do this the easy way, where you tell me what it is I want to know willingly, or the hard way, where you get as much pain as humanly possible, without killing you can be inflicted, and you still tell me what I want to know. Understand, and above all, believe that when you make your choice, you'll be stuck until the end. So, answer up."

CHAPTER ELEVEN

The name they gave me was a name I'd thought I'd never hear again. A name from back in middle school when I was going to Havenview Middle. Angie Carson.

Also known as Carson City, she was from South Memphis, right on the edges of Da Haven. We went to the same school because it was for the whole Haven, being the only school for Oakhaven and Whitehaven to share between them.

Angie was a white bitch way out by the tracks with some type of family connection, but she was always in the mix. She stood about 5'5" with the body of an exotic dancer. Not your typical white girl at all. She stayed fighting 'cause she knew that as long as she had the shadow of her family over her, nobody would respect her name and brand. What made it worse for her was that she was blond-haired, blue-eyed, 100% white bread. I had one run-in with the bitch during my first year of middle school. She heard I was tied in with family but was doing my own thing in the hustle. We were halfway through the school year when I caught wind that she had it in for me and was going to try me out.

I didn't even let her have the satisfaction of surprise. I went looking for her right after school and found her walking off campus. No words. Just walked up to her and slapped the shit out of her, so it wasn't any doubt of why I was there. When she went to put her hands up after snapping to what was happening, I went to work like the old films of Laila Ali. She shocked me by standing tall and going toe to toe with me for a second.

I admit, she could take a punch, and she was pissing me off, not falling. It wasn't until I got her with a nicely timed hook to the jaw that she aborted the mission and went for the famous hair pull. Seeing her coming, I stepped into a kick that left her sitting on her ass, holding her stomach, and trying to catch the breath that just left her lungs.

After that, Angie never fucked with me again, nor did I fuck with her. I went on about my business and figured she went about the same. What irked me to the highest degree was that I met Tasha and Ivy that same year.

This led me to the non-coincident visit by my uncle and cousin. That meant Papi was a step ahead of me in finding out who was behind all this truly disturbing situation. Her wanting to take over my area of business in adult entertainment meant she had her family's blessing. So, my problem had become my family's problem at the end of this.

When I got Papi on the phone, I called him out on it, and he confirmed everything from his stepping back into his role in the family to momma reaching out to her old crew of family. I wondered that while Papi's own car was the lone occupant of the yard today, my uncle and cousin were there, seemingly settled for a long stay.

Everybody had to check on their information grapevines to figure out just how deep her claws were into the whole Haven area. Oakhaven only had one majority crew in its section: M.A.C. Mafia. I just had businesses and was just opening the trap spots around the hood, so I wasn't big. Before M.A.C. Mafia, Papi ran Oakhaven. He didn't care about who wanted to make money 'cause he felt it was enough for everybody to eat. Whitehaven, out by the tracks, had to share ground with Graceland because that was what that area was recognized as.

Cat Daddy gave me all the information on Angie's mob ties. He kept his ears on most major players in the city 'cause he had done work for most of them. He offered to see if he could arrange a sit down for me to have with Angie and her father, along with Papi. I, on the other hand, had to deal with the waste still in the auto shop with me.

All four remained tied up in the middle of the floor, but it was Tasha and Ivy who was not going to make it out of there at all. I planned on utilizing Capone and DiVinci's services until I was paid in full. After that, who was to say what would happen. In the meantime, they had to stay under wraps until the end of this situation. The circumstances that led to this point of my Bullshit Festival wasn't even a blip on my radar anywhere. If the bitch had it like that in her heart with hate for me because the bitch had my name in her mouth about

take care of them for me and call when you done."

As they moved in tandem to carry out their task as requested, I turned around, only to be face-to-face with D-Wild. He was smiling like a proud father, and then he turned serious. He stuck his hand out, motioning for the pistol in my hand. As I gave it to him, he held onto my hand for the briefest second, knowing. My face must have betrayed my act of courage, showing I was actually nervous. Even though it was necessary, I would never get used to taking the life of another, and he must have seen that in me. He walked away from me and handed the gun to A1, who tucked it in his waist.

"Good news and bad news," Cat Daddy said, announcing his presence and receiving my attention. "Which one you want first?"

"Good news, then follow with the bad news," I answered warily.

"The sit down is arranged to meet downtown at the riverside park," he informed me. "The thing is, it's in half an hour, which means you have to leave now in order to get there on time."

"Damn!" I cussed, thinking fast. "Okay, since Kyle brought his truck, why don't you, Dorian, Kayla, and him ride out behind me, and D-Wild rides with me?" '

"Sounds like a plan," Cat Daddy responded.

After informing everybody what was next, I made a dash to my 745. D-Wild ran past me to open the gate. As I pulled out, he jumped in with a smile on his face. I wanted to ask what the smile was for, but I decided to go another route.

I let my mind wonder about the sit-down and what could possibly come of it. Though Angie didn't have a direct hand in my situation, she was the one who planted the seed in the minds of Tasha and Ivy to get me out the way. The fact that they wasn't part of the Carson Family Mob, or Carson City Cartel, headed by Angie, meant that there could be a total displeasure in this meeting by me pointing out that Angie advised them. I knew all the talk that was coming and needed to prepare for their arguments with a focused mind.

A little under half an hour later, I pulled into the parking lot of the riverside park. The whole way there, Kyle was on my heels in his truck like I had a trailer hitched to my car. Pulling into a parking space, I scanned the part of the park that led downhill toward the water to see if I could spot anybody. Stepping out of the car, the smell of the Mississippi River invaded my nose.

"I see Papi," D-Wild announced.

When I looked at him, he pointed back in the direction to my left. I turned to catch sight of him. When I did, I noticed there were two people with him. After my earlier visit, I knew it was Uncle E and Miguel with Papi. The seriousness of this meeting didn't evade me, but seeing Papi with Uncle E and Miguel displayed exactly how serious this was.

"Envy, when they see you coming, all the people not directly part of the meeting will break off and watch the surroundings and each other's guards," Cat Daddy familiarized me on the formalities. "The only advice I have for you during the meeting is to show backbone. Meaning, be your 'Boss Bitch' self and don't fold unless absolutely necessary."

"Okay, let's get this show on the road," I uttered, mostly to myself, and began walking in Papi's direction.

Accurately with Cat Daddy's words, as soon as Uncle E and Miguel spotted me, they said something to Papi and broke off, breaking off and heading in my direction. That was when I noticed the white men standing around and forming into one group. From the group, a man and woman walked towards Papi. There were no words traded as Uncle E and Miguel walked past me and linked up with Cat Daddy and the others.

Getting closer, Angie was saying something, but I wasn't close enough to hear what. When I came close enough, Papi gave me a nod, but it was the old white man who spoke.

"You must obviously be Envy," the man said with a look on his face. "You asked for this sit-down in the nature of..." he said, leaving the sentence hanging.

"Don't be rude, Car..." Papi said before I cut in.

"No, Papi, I got it. Trust me," I said with a smile. Then my face went blank as I faced old crusty. "Yeah, I'm Envy, and this is Papi. I know Angie or Carson City, but I fail to know who you are and your place. This sit-down can and will turn into a walk-off if we can't respect each other. So, since you know who I am, who are you?"

The man looked stunned that I spoke so freely to him, letting me know he was used to giving orders out and them being followed to the letter.

Angie moved forward to speak, but the man's hand landing on her shoulder brought her to a halt.

"Fair enough, I guess," he said. "I'm Poppa Carson, head of the Carson Family and the father of Angie, who is head of Carson City Cartel."

"Nice to meet you, Poppa Carson," I greeted him, unmoved. "I'm Envy Santiago of the 220/221 Hustle Mafia Family, and daughter of Papi Santiago, head of the Santiago Cartel."

"Okay, now that we've got the pleasantries out of the way," Poppa Carson started. "Can we hear what this is all about? Because I have no idea what this is about."

As I explained from the beginning about the murder charge and ended with me receiving Angie's name as the one who advised the problem, I could see that Poppa Carson was going to defend Angie like she was innocent of any wrongdoing. When I started to detail why I figured Angie had it in for me, because of our past beef and her wanting to take over the area I was in, Papa Clark looked at Angie, who, in turn, looked at me and cut me off.

"First of all, Envy, them hoes ain't part of nothing I have going on, or my father," Angie said sharply. "So, what they did had nothing to do with any of us. Now, as far as that neighborhood goes, Papi retired, leaving it open for anybody to reign supreme."

When she finished, I gave her a shark smile, all teeth. The bitch thought she was smart and the most clever person ever to play the game. It was my job to bring her entitled ass down to size in such a fashion that it would leave no question as to where I stood on the problem and future events should they arise.

"I figured that you would say as much, so let me clear the air and wipe the slate clean so we can start over," I began, gaining traction with my words. "Oakhaven is not open for anybody anymore. As far as I understood, Papi handed the reigns to his protege, who is head of M.A.C. Mafia, so it was never open in the first place. Secondly, 220/221 Hustle Mafia Family is stepping into the game and already has a foot planted deep in the hood like the roots of an oak tree. The Hustle Mafia Family has crews from both sides of the Haven area, so be happy I don't want the tracks that y'all control." I looked from Poppa Carson to Angie, letting the statement gain ground before I continued.

"From Orange Mound to Whitehaven is part of my organization. I only want to remain in my lane, but I know how to drive reckless and swerve into others' lanes as a defensive driver. Even though Papi is here, you can act as if he is invisible because what I have going on has nothing to do with him at all except the fact that I'm his daughter," I said, making myself clear. "Other than that, he is an ally only if needed, but I handle my own business and problems. What I had hoped to gain from this meeting was understanding and respect because I went through the proper channels instead of acting on the information I received. So, now I'll say this, and I'm done. Stay out of my way, and I'll stay out of yours. I don't want any problems, but I'm not afraid to take necessary action to solve a problem accordingly."

Poppa Carson looked at Papi, smiled, and then laughed. When I looked at Papi, he was looking at his nails like they were the most fascinating thing he had ever seen.

"Santiago, if this is your daughter, then I'd hate for you to have a son," Poppa Carson said between laughs, turning red in the face. "Envy, let me make something perfectly clear to you, honey. If I didn't know your father, I would take your little speech as disrespect and a potential threat. That being said, I like your heart that has just been showing, and I respect that you have your own voice."

When I didn't speak, he continued more seriously, "From what you've said so far is that you've got the word of two, quote-unquote, snitches who implicated that Angie advised them to snitch on you." He cocked his hand to the side, showing that he felt I should be smarter about the situation. "Now, I'm not saying she did or didn't, but regardless of it, she didn't have any direct involvement. They are not a part of either of our organizations, so--"

"No disrespect, but I've had enough of this bullshit," I said aggressively, cutting Poppa Carson off. "Frankly, I expected as much to come out of this whole situation." I looked at Angie, letting her see the fire that was burning inside of me, which I was controlling. "That's why I recorded everything that was said. Now Angie, before your pops tries to dispute this in your defense, I'm going to play this for all of us to hear, and then I will erase it from existence. Lastly, I don't respect that while this is actually between us, you have your father speaking for you. So, continue to remain quiet under your pop's protection as this plays."

"This should be interesting," Papi said, intrigued.

As I pulled my phone out, there was movement. I looked up to see Poppa Carson holding Angie by the shoulders.

"I want to hear this," Poppa Carson said to Angie, who stared at me with a hate I had never seen in eyes before.

****

"You need to be sure about what you say next, Tasha," my voice came out of the phone speaker.

"Angie Carson told us to get you out the way, and she would make us a part of her crew," Tasha's voice rang out. "When you got out, she said to burn your business down 'cause she was ready to take over the hood and your business."

"So, you telling me that you bitches was working with Ms. Carson City?" I heard myself ask. "You turned on me to ride with a bitch I had a middle school beef with?"

"You wasn't fucking with us no more, and Angie said she would put us on with her and put us on our money," Ivy could be heard saying. "We had Orange Mound Money Gang with us, but they ain't know nothing about what was going on."

"We was gon' leave they ass high and dry when we became a part of Carson City Cartel. That was the plan after you got out," Tasha added. "Envy, please don't tell her we told you. She'll have us killed if she found out we talked to you."

****

Poppa Carson looked from me to Angie as the recording ended but remained quiet.

"Seeing as this situation is the way it is, Carson, you and I need to step off to the side and have a discussion," Papi broke his silence. "We've done a lot of business together over the years, but being as your daughter and my daughter are possibly embarking on the edge of a potential war, it's imperative we make preparations to conclude our business dealings."

Neither said a word as they stepped off to the side. However, Poppa Carson looked at Angie with disapproval, revealing that he had no idea about his daughter's dealings. The look on his face when his eyes turned to me let me know that Papi was right. Regardless of what happened after this, Poppa Carson would stand behind his daughter, whether right or wrong.

When Papi and Poppa Carson began their conversation, I turned my attention to Angie, wondering what would happen next.

"I don't know what disappoints me more about this," I started off with. "The fact that a trivial mixup between us in middle school has us here, the fact that you couldn't deal with me on your own, or that instead of being a woman, you sit there like a little girl letting your pops speak for you. Are you telling me that all that fighting you did coming up, you still are in his shadow and not on your own two toes?"

"My pop is stuck in the old ways and believes I should be as well," Angie told me, her face twisted and red. "I, on the other hand, believe that the whole city is open for us. I have no allegiances except for those of family." Her face relaxed, and I noticed she wasn't finished, so I remained quiet. "I'll be honest. At first, I didn't know they were speaking about you when they first came out. It wasn't until you got out that they finally spoke your name. From there, I knew it wasn't any going back. I'm an adamant believer that if you start something, finish it. You were clever in arranging a meeting with our respective families and bringing this out, so now there are no more shadows to hide in. I'm assuming that Tasha and Ivy have been taken care of already?"

"Look, enough of the sideways talk. What needs to be understood right now is where you stand. Are we gon' dead this, or do we both have to be on high alert?" I asked, annoyed. "Before you answer, let me say that I stand by what I said earlier about staying in my own lane as long as I receive the same respect."

"Your problem is you feel since you Papi's daughter that you better than everybody else," Angie began, but I couldn't let her finish that statement.

"See, I'm tired of this shit with you bitches feeling that way, so let me make something very clear," I interrupted with my voice low and menacingly. "I don't feel I'm better than nobody, but I do keep a chip on my shoulder because I don't want the shadow of Papi hanging over me like you got your pop's over you. Hint the reason why I formed my own shit without a family backing my every move. That's the difference between you and me, and the bigger one, I might add. Papi doesn't speak for me when it comes to my business. Had it been to Poppa Carson, he would still be right here speaking to me for you. So, your spoonfed, entitled ass can kill that high horse speech and make a decision for yourself before your daddy comes back over here and make it for you, little girl."

I clearly struck a nerve because Angie's face went from

relaxed back to tense. I couldn't care less about her feelings on what I said. It was true. While she was still using her pops as a platform, I had branched off to do my own building so I could be respected as my own. A Boss Bitch, born, bred, and to the death of me. I didn't respect her. I understood why Cat Daddy included Papi, and I made it clear that even though he was present, he was not a participating party in my operations at all. So, from the beginning, I distanced myself as an independent while she remained quiet, resolving to be a subordinate to her father, letting him speak for her.

In response to my question and speech, Angie turned her back and walked away from the conversation, giving me her answer on how to proceed. Seeing his daughter leaving, Poppa Carson and Papi walked toward me. Before they reached me, I turned in time to watch Angie and her guards enter a vehicle and leave.

"What's the word, Envy?" Papi asked me.

"That was her answer," I answered simply, already preparing moves in my head.

"There will not be a war, and I'll make sure to tell her that," Poppa Carson assured me confidently.

"That's not up to you. Even though I respect your offer," I said respectfully. "She has her mind set on it, regardless of what you say. She expects to be backed by you because you spoiled her Poppa Carson." I turned and looked him in the eyes. "I understand the position this puts you and Papi in, and if I could change it, I would. I'm about making money and building. This is sure to cause a lot of heartache, grief, and financial problems for all involved. Now, if you would excuse me, it was nice meeting you. Wish it was under better circumstances."

I walked away, leaving Papi and Poppa Carson standing alone. My thoughts had already moved on to how to defend in the upcoming war.

When I reached the group of D-Wild, Dorian, Kyle, Kayla, Cat Daddy, Uncle E, and Miguel, they looked at me questioningly. I remained silent, looking at everyone one at a time.

"That bad, huh?" Uncle E questioned.

"Tell us at least you solved a little of the problem," Miguel said.

When I didn't respond immediately, D-Wild stepped up to me and put his hand on my shoulder. He dipped his head to make eye contact with me. When I looked into his eyes, my decision became solid.

"Shit is about to get real, and it's going to be hell," I said in a leveled tone. "If you don't want to be part of any of this, then this is the time to walk away."

"Ma, when you was having your talk, we had one of our own," D-Wild told me with a serious look. "Whatever happened over there, we was and are going to stand beside you and behind you."

"Yeah, Envy, D-Wild got M.A.C. Mafia with him, and I called my brother," Dorian informed me. "He said all I got to do is say the word, and Blackhaven Gorillas will come like mad Russians."

When I looked at Kayla, she responded simply, "Bitch please!" and Kyle folded his arms across his chest.

It wasn't until Cat Daddy spoke up that I felt better.

"Envy, Envy, Envy," Cat Daddy said sternly. "I didn't believe it was in any way necessary that you would have to question loyalty from me." He then smiled. "If this wasn't a neutral and peaceful meeting, your problem would have been solved ten minutes ago. Poppa Carson and his daughter would be down and us gone from the scene. Now, if you'll please continue to inform us, we'll move forward."

Knowing where Uncle E and Miguel stood on this, I didn't even bother to look in their direction.

"Her answer to the solution was to walk away. Poppa Carson doesn't want problems, but by her being his daughter, we know the outcome," I informed everyone. "We a small group, and they outnumber and outgun us by a large number. Be sure of everyone who will be a part of us and this... 'cause, as of now, we are to be on high alert from here on out. We'll let them make the first move. Once that happens, then we go straight for the head and be done with it. We not gon' drag this out 'cause that means we not making money." I looked at Uncle E and Miguel. "I'm sorry y'all got pulled into this, and tell Papi I'll call him later."

CHAPTER TWELVE

The sudden onslaught of rain that took over the skies and the clouds that threw a dark tint over the earth was a welcomed addition to my day. The storm was a cartoon copy of the emotions and thoughts swirling inside of me. It also brought along with it a sense of calm that could soothe with its symphony of sound.

Pulling into a parking space in front of Platinum Services, my thoughts went to the lessons Papi and Cat Daddy gave me on the game of chess. Every move made had a purpose that would lead to the success or failure of whatever was being attempted. Defense was to be built first before an offense was put into motion because if you move to offense without a defense, the game could end in a slaughter. Everyone played differently. Papi was more reserved in the finesse of his moves and game, whereas Cat Daddy's finesse was more aggressive. Their minds were different, but they were the exact same when it came to the cause of their moves.

"Envy," D-Wild spoke from the passenger seat. "You

good? You zoned out on me."

"Just thinking," I said, looking into his face. He had a concerned look that caused me to want to ease his mind. "D, I don't know how long it's going to take to resolve all that's going on, but what I do know is this. Every move counts, and each move will take considerable thought. We need to be on our A+ game, firing on all cylinders. Nothing can be done on impulse or compulsively. For every action, there is a reaction. So, if we gon' roll the dice, I want to make sure we don't crap out on the first roll."

Kyle's truck pulled in beside me as D-Wild began to answer.

"Just remember this one thing, and I'll make myself scarce so you can focus." When I nodded, he continued, "You got back up, so don't keep shit too close to your chest. Now, I'm bout to make some calls and let my niggas know the alliances that have been set and the marked enemy."

He didn't wait for my response as he got out of the car. I watched as he closed the door and made his way into Platinum Services. As if on cue, T.I. played on my phone, telling me to stand up.

"What's up, Cat Daddy?" I answered the phone, looking at Kyle's truck. "You didn't have to call. You coulda got in with me."

"Well, if I was where you are, I would, but seeing as I'm not, I decided to ring your line," he informed me.

"Okay, talk to me," I replied, curious to know what was going on.

"There's somebody I want you to meet," Cat Daddy

started. "He a good nigga, and he rides with me and my brothers every now and then. He's an independent with no ties to anybody except maybe yours truly."

"I trust your judgment, but that ain't why you telling me this," I remarked questioningly. "So, stop procrastinating, please."

To my surprise, Cat Daddy ended his usual banter and began informing me on his friend, a dude named Easy Money, who was an all-around hustler from washing cars to murder for hire. Cat Daddy only knew everything about him because he raised and schooled him in the art of being a hustler. He was truly an independent who didn't participate in the politics of the ghetto, but when judgment was passed and a sentence needed to be carried out, he didn't hesitate. Nobody knew about him because Cat Daddy would pass work to him and let him handle it on his own accord without interference.

On the other hand, Easy Money's drug game and pimping was notorious around Memphis. He worked his way up in the game from the tender age of twelve after he ran away from home and eventually ran into Cat Daddy and his twin Money Mike before Sir Brit became part of the trio. Easy Money became a silent partner after that. He got his name because after an objective was complete, he would always celebrate with four words: "That was easy money."

He'd been riding with Cat Daddy for all of ten years, but in the fifth year, he decided to build himself separately from the brothers. They remained close in the last five years and in constant contact. Cat Daddy then told me that he contacted him to throw his hat in with us, and Easy Money accepted with one condition. I would learn the condition by meeting with him. When I told Cat Daddy to bring him over, he told me it would be better if I drove to them.

After receiving the meeting place information, I started my car and proceeded to leave Platinum Services. Before hanging up, Cat Daddy assured me that it wouldn't be a waste of time for me to travel to Cordova, where they were. Cordova was about forty-five minutes to an hour outside Memphis on the other side of Barlett. I put the info in my GPS and headed in that direction.

Leaving the storm assaulting Memphis behind me, my mind was clearing up but still as cloudy as the sky overhead. It wasn't until I passed all the way through Barlett that the rain ceased to shower my windshield, leaving me with a clear sight of the path that lay before me, both figuratively and literally.

Thoughts became pieced together, and a plan was formulated as I reached my destination. When I pulled up to the long driveway with trees running along both sides and a large open yard on either side of those, I couldn't help but notice the sign on the fence surrounding the property. "Fuck the dog! Beware of the owner!" signs are on the fence opening and on a tree on my driver's side. I smirked at the sight of them, keeping my mind open for who I was about to meet.

Knowing I was invited, I pulled up to the fence and saw an intercom and button to push. Before I could roll my window down, the fence opened automatically. I paused for a second, looking for the camera that was obviously somewhere in the vicinity. Not spotting it at first glance, I drove up the driveway. Rounding a curve, I came into a clearing where a very modest one-story house sat by itself, and I saw another small building a little ways off from the main house.

On the side of the main house was a two-door garage painted in a mint-green, matching the house, with a truck parked in front of it. Upon further notice, the truck was a Chevy Silverado painted a glossy black on black rims, giving it a menacing look. In front of the house was Cat Daddy's money-green Caprice, which calmed me. Pulling beside the Caprice, the front door opened, and Sir Brit appeared.

Getting out of the car and closing the door, I was welcomed with two barks that spun me around. I turned to face an enormous jet-black Pitbull standing with its tongue out and tail wagging. It wasn't until the Pitbull approached me and licked my hand that I relaxed. As if sensing the change in me, the Pitbull turned to leave. It looked back when I still stood there. It barked, still facing away from me, and I took that as the Pitbull communicating for me to follow it. I complied, and the Pitbull led the way to the front door, where Sir Brit was waiting with a smile.

"I was told not to interfere with you and Smoke's introduction," he said as an explanation. "As a dog, he has a great sense of judging character like his owner."

When I didn't respond, his smile disappeared and was replaced with a seriousness I didn't usually see from him.

"Easy Money wanted to get your reaction to Smoke being your welcoming committee to his home," Sir Britt said, stepping back into the house.

I stepped into the house and turned to close the door.

"You can leave it open. I usually do," a voice said from my right.

I turned to see Cat Daddy, Money Mike, and the dude I perceived to be Easy Money seated in separate chairs around a large room off to the right of the front door with windows looking out into the front of the house and a Big 1500 inch flatscreen connected to the ceiling at an angle.

Everything on the screen was an overhead view of the property.

"Envy, this is Easy Money," Cat Daddy began as an introduction.

"Envy," Easy Money eased out. "Nice to meet you."

He stood to his feet. He looked to be 5'5" -5'6" of pure dope boy classic. He was a dark brother with tight cornrows. A pair of rocks in his ears screamed, "Paid." On his neck was a thumb-thick platinum chain with a diamond-encrusted platinum "E$" hanging from it. He wore a black muscle shirt that showed the tattoos that covered his slightly muscular frame of a boxer. He also wore black jean shorts with the Gucci belt and a pair of all-black retro Jordans on his feet.

His approach was so smooth it was as if he moved to a rhythm only he could hear as he reached out his hand to shake mine.

"Likewise," I responded as I took his hand in mine.

"I'm pleased you could make it. Pimpin' told me about the situation and his role in it as a whole. I know for him to be completely committed to the cause, there must be an imperative and meaningful reason," Easy Money said, looking me in the eyes. "When he reached out to me, I told him I must meet you. See, I also knew your father. I won't say in what capacity because that would take the majority of the day. Let me ask you a question or two if that's alright with you."

I nodded for him to continue.

"Cool, let's take a seat," he said as he motioned toward the seat he had occupied when I walked in. He decided to stand, and I wondered why he didn't take a seat in the fifth chair to my left. "I'll just throw both questions at once so I won't have to interrupt your full and complete response. Okay, first, what is your ultimate cause in this life? 'Cause I know, for a fact, you don't have to participate in street politics or activities. Second, what makes you different from the rest who want all-out total dominance over others? Because there is dominance in play at the end of the day. Please, when you answer, speak from your heart."

Before I began to respond, he grabbed the remote from the coffee table in the middle of the room and pressed a button. On the TV screen, different angles of the property were shown. He pressed another button, and the wall behind me slid to the side, revealing a room with a dozen computer screens. However, it was what graced the left wall that garnered attention. There was an organized display of firearms in rows. Then he must have pressed another button because Yo Gotti's "I AM" album began to play softly throughout the room from hidden speakers.

"I must admit that I was highly impressed. You don't

understand how much you put me into my element," I remarked. "Can a lady get a drink and something to smoke?"

"I hoped you would appreciate understanding who you were becoming acquainted with and know that regardless if I joined in your cause or not, I'm well equipped to do my part," he gave me a smile. "Whatever my role may be, regardless if I'm on the sidelines as a safehouse or a soldier in the army."

He was correct in his analysis of my appreciation of his presentation. I learned as much as I needed to from his preparation and security. He would be an exceptional ally to acquire if he accepted putting his bid in with us. I couldn't let him not be an ally or part of the organization, so my next words had to rival what I was introduced to by him.

By way of answer to my request for a drink and smoke, Easy Money walked to a small refrigerator that sat off the corner of the room. As he fixed my drink, Cat Daddy handed me a lit blunt. I gave him a nod of thanks and took a strong pull of the strong-scented Mary Jane. Easy Money returned to me with an amber liquid in a square glass and two cubes of ice.

"Jack on the rocks with a splash of coke," he stated.

"Thank you," I accepted the drink courteously. "Okay, I'll answer your questions now. Bear with me." I took a sip of the drink, and it was mixed perfectly. I looked at the drink, then at him appreciatively, and began. "Before beginning to form an organization, I was completely focused on operating a business enterprise. The small circle I associated with had their position and jobs. As my business grew, so did all of our wages. You can say we were reviewing equal wages because most of my finances went back into my business. I built up from there and spread the wealth as well as my businesses. Everyone with me is here by choice and can branch out to do their own things and stay a part of the business or even open under my business head, Platinum Services."

I took another pull of the herb and held it in while I took a good sip of my drink before continuing, "Even now, after wanting to form an organized family of bosses, I still have that mentality. I'm all for growth and don't want to have the spotlight directly on me. I am the head chair, but there is equal say amongst a select few that form the brain of this. Cat Daddy can attest to that, being the one to suggest and implement himself and having four others stand beside me. I summarize with this..." I looked straight at him, needing him to hear me.

"I'm a Boss Bitch that loves to be around those of a like mind with shared goals. I want to be able to learn from those who sit at the table with me, as well as having those around me learn from me. Steel sharpens steel if you know what I mean. Plus, the gold standard on the side with a tough grill, my guy."

Easy Money looked at Cat Daddy for a brief second. Then, the slightest smile presented his face. He then looked me back in the eyes.

"Pimpin, you said she was the shit, but you ain't tell me she was with the shit," Easy Money said playfully. "So, he really did school you on game and hustle. I know Papi gave you a jewel or two, but I see the gems that Pimpin influenced you in on, Envy." He looked back to Cat Daddy, asking, "How much did you school her with?"

"That's it," Cat Daddy answered. "Never beyond money."

"If you speaking in my shoulder game or smoking aim, I'm self-taught," I remarked, catching the words. "I ain't perfect, but I'm decent enough to knock a nigga, or bitch, dick in the dirt if need be."

"Well, Madame, I think I may just take a ride in the car with you. Just know, zero to a hundred in two point two seconds isn't necessarily good," he said as he reached into his pocket. From his pocket, he pulled a set of keys and a cord. "Here's a condition. You take this property as my investment and move in. Security will be my department, and I'll make this my first act of work."

"You want me to move in with you?" I asked curiously.

"No, this will be yours," Easy Money answered. "When Pimpin told me the business, I knew that if you proved your worth in words, you'd need to be properly protected. So, I decided to slide this to you as a gift once I agreed to put in with you. This is just one of my properties. This one is the only one close enough to Memphis that isn't my home."

"He uses it as a duck off for all of us," Cat Daddy informed me. "He got another further up the road, about thirty minutes away. So, we'll be alright."

"I also know about D-Wild as well," Easy Money said. "So, I know you hands-off as family. Family by Pimpin and love of money," he paused in thought. "220/221 Hustle Mafia Family? That's a long name, ain't it?"

"You could use either or the other because it's one and the

same. 220 identifies the men, and 221 identifies the women. Hustle Mafia Family is the whole," I explained. "220 means second to none, and 221 is second to no one."

Easy Money chuckled goodnaturedly, then said, "I like you, and I don't like many people. Respect, yes. Like, no." He turned and headed to the small fridge. "I believe this calls for a toast to commemorate the joining of this union."

He pulled out the bottle of Jack Daniels and closed the fridge. He walked to the office table in silence and grabbed his glass, filling it halfway. When he was done, he made his way around the room, starting with Sir Brit and ending with me. Each person stood after their glass was filled, so I followed suit. Easy Money gave a quick sharp whistle, and Smoke ran in from outside soon after with his tail wagging happily.

"Envy, this is essentially for the benefit of your knowing. They," he began, gesturing to the brothers, "already know that my word is like the second part of my name. Seeing as you are being introduced to me for the first time, I deem this to be necessary to eliminate any doubt of my allegiance to your movement."

He raised his glass up. We did the same as he continued.

"We are here to merge minds and forge a unification that relies on shared goals, trust, and loyalty of all parties involved. I will meet the others in due time, but as of this moment, you represent those not present. So, through you, from me, please forward my next words. I submit my application and resume to the cause that is 220/221 Hustle Mafia Family. I will fulfill my role as a part of this organization and protect it against anyone set against it. To family."

"To family," we all repeated as one and drank to officially become whole.

"That was beautiful, Easy Money," Cat Daddy expressed with a smile.

"Well, I learned from an educated man that words carry weight and shouldn't be presented as a hollow object," Easy Money responded with his own smile. "We all should understand the significance of one's words spoken to another human being. Though it is said that actions speak louder than words, the words set the tone and standard for the quality and quantity of action."

I was in awe at his choice of words and the wisdom he graced the room with at that moment. There was a question in need of an answer.

"How old are you, Easy Money, if you don't mind me asking?" I asked.

"Not at all," his response confident. "I just turned 22 a couple of weeks ago."

"It's safe to say that knowledge, wisdom, and understanding don't care about the age of the person receiving them. Only the willingness to gain, obtain, sustain, and maintain an interpretation of the lessons and jewels given," I remarked as I took a pull of the blunt still in my possession. "I believe that this has become the beginning of a beautiful relationship. You won't be disappointed with the ride we will be embarking together on this journey that lies before us, Easy Money."

"Indeed," he responded, then became quiet before

continuing seriously. "Now, on the business of your current complication. I understand that you want to play it by ear. May I make a suggestion?"

I shrugged my shoulders in consent.

"Okay. First, let me say that I know the Carsons and have done some work for them. Poppa Carson got connections here and in Texas, Louisiana, Mississippi, Alabama, Georgia, and South Carolina. He got family in Arkansas that are Klansmen who he visually gets his firearms from. Poppa Carson himself is a closet racist, but he can't show it because he does business with so many races that if it came out, he would cease to be relevant and become a permanent enemy of most of his partners," Easy Money enlightened. "I say to say this. His daughter Angie doesn't have the same problem as he does because her organization lets her stance on race relations be known. My suggestion is to hurt them with this information. I don't even believe Papi knows the depth of what I'm explaining. If he did, he wouldn't have done any type of business with him."

"What will exposing his racism accomplish?" I asked curiously.

"Get to their connections that are outside their race, causing them to lose their grip in the city and force them to leave. Hopefully," Easy Money said confidently. "Angie loses her organization and has to fully represent Carson Family, revealing the ugly truth."

"After listening to you, I think I've got a better idea. It's a little devious, but it'll bear the same result," I said with a smile. "Tell me what you think about this."

CHAPTER THIRTEEN

After giving my idea a shot and tweaking it with different ideas from everyone, the decision was made on the avenue of action to be taken. At the end of the planning, Easy Money looked at me and said he'd hate to be my enemy if I could think like I did.

On the way back to Memphis, the skies cleared of dark clouds and rain and left a scent that was so refreshing. Easy Money agreed to meet with everyone who stayed on. I was going to find out because they were all at Platinum Services waiting for me to get there. During the drive, I received two calls.

The first was from Momma, letting me know she had some Rastas close at hand just in case. Her voice was so thick with her Jamaican accent that she reverted to her native tongue of Patois several times. The second call came from D-Wild, who informed me that the situation was relayed to everyone. Dorian called his brother and confirmed things with him while Kyle spoke to his homeboys. D-Wild himself told me that he had a conference call with the other heads of M.A.C. Mafia, and they were on board, relying on his judgment. I would find out about everyone else when I got there.

I was ten minutes away from Platinum Services when my phone rang with the default ringtone I had set for unknown numbers. It was on an in-town number, but for it not to be locked in my phone confused me. I hit ignore and continued on the way to the office.

When the phone rang again, I got a bad feeling in the pit of my stomach. I looked at the phone again, racking my brain and wondering who had my number that I failed to lock in. I decided to find out since the hint wasn't taken the first time I sent them to voicemail.

"Hello?" I answered the phone.

"Envy, you are one hard person to catch up with," a familiar voice came through my speakers, saying, the accent light enough to miss. "If I didn't know any better, I would think you didn't love me no more."

A flood of emotion coursed through me that I hadn't felt in a long time until D-Wild came into my life. Memories invaded me of the days when I was just figuring out who I wanted to be and how I wanted to become that person.

Rudolph Brown, best known as Lil Ru, was my first. The time we were together, he was a one-man wrecking crew that was building his own name. Lil Ru was the epitome of a young gangsta. So much so that he caught his first body at age 15 and his first charge at 17. I hung with him, hoping

DEREK BROWN

he'd slow down, but he didn't. So, when he got out and wasn't trying to move a safer, profitable route, I made a choice that I knew would hurt but had to be done in order to elevate. He told me he understood and didn't hold it against me. Last time I heard anything about him was six years ago when he went down on a robbery charge. I thought all feelings were erased.

Guess not.

This Latino brother was as suave as they came and as ruthless. Papi even warned me away from him. He told me that Lil Ru was more of a hoodlum than a business-caliber nigga. The rest was history.

"I would ask how you got my number, but that would be a waste of time," I said with a laugh. "I can't say I ain't happy to hear from you, though. When you get out, Ru?"

"I got out a couple days ago. How I got your number will surprise you like it did me," Lil Ru responded. "Yo pops reached out to my cousin Dago, asking for information about a couple of things. I heard him say Papi and told Dago to greet him for me. Instead of it being left at that, Papi asked to holler at me."

"So, he gave you my number, huh?" I asked in wonder.

"That and the fact that you had a situation going on and you formed your own family," Lil Ru answered, confirming my next question. "He also let me know about D-Wild after I asked if you were seeing anybody."

I heard the tone of his voice change ever so slightly as he made his last comment. As a couple, we were a beast. If he fought a nigga and they had a female with them, I made sure to bring the bitch into the fight, showing that he had a down-by-law bitch on his team. He got to the point that it was a foregone conclusion, and expectation, that if a bitch rode with the nigga that was beefing with Lil Ru, she might as well square up and beat me to the punch. Seldom happened, though, 'cause I stayed on the lookout for the bitches.

"Yeah, me and D-Wild been riding for a little while now. He's also a partner in the family," I said, easing off the subject to kill the awkwardness of it. "How much did Papi give you on what's going on?"

"Enough for me to understand that you need as many people as you can trust beside you and behind you," Lil Ru told me. "You know I ride solo, except for with my cousin and a few of his niggas every now and then. So, if you need or want me, I'm extending my hand out to assist you in any way."

If Lil Ru wasn't my ex, I wouldn't have needed time to think about him helping me at all. I didn't want it to be uncomfortable for me or anybody else.

"If you worried, Papi already talked to D-Wild and had me on three-way," Lil Ru shocked me by saying. "When I asked if I could help, he said it would be better to talk to you. He also said he was secure enough to know his place and hoped I would, too."

Yep, that sounded like D-Wild. I couldn't help my laugh escaping me. I felt a relief that it was already out in the open.

"If he said that, then why don't you meet me at my office?" I said, decision made. "It's in the storefront of Winchester and Tchoulohoma called Platinum Services."

"I know," he said simply. "I'm already here."

I damn near ran the red light. I was in so much shock. I was looking at Platinum Services from the light, trying to figure out what to make of what just transpired while I was meeting with Easy Money. D-Wild could have told me what was up, and I was sure as shit gon' give him an ear full when I got there.

I hung up the line without a response, hoping to cause some nervousness in him that I felt myself. When the light turned green, I slowly pulled off and then had a better idea as I pressed the accelerator, causing the 745 to jerk in response.

I pulled into the parking lot like a bat out of hell, formulating a way to get at these two niggas. Whether they knew it or not, they opened a door I wouldn't let close. I was wondering who would catch on to my antics first and call me out on it as I pulled into a parking space.

I got out of the car, closed the door, and powerwalked to the glass doors. I yanked the doors open, but whatever my plan was... it dissolved when I seen all the people were in the office.

It wasn't until my eyes rested on Lil Ru that I got over my initial shock. He aged well and had a growth spurt since I last laid eyes on him. He looked to be six feet or better. His hazel brown eyes sat in the middle of a pretty boy face. He wore a fitted hat over his shoulder-length black hair. He wore a chin strap goatee and beard that gave him a more mature look. Prison did wonders for his body. His white v-neck t-shirt hugged his torso, showing the contours of his physique, clearly shaped from a dedicated workout. The blue jeans shorts he wore had the Gucci symbols imprinted faintly all over, also showing strong legs leading to the black ankle socks that were covered by ice white shell toe Adidas. The only piece of jewelry he wore was a gold watch on his wrist, and no tattoos were visible.

"Nigga, you slicker than a snake in a can full of oil!" I snapped back in character. "And D-Wild, you think you flyer than a New Orleans Pelican right now, don't you?" I didn't let either of them respond before I continued. "Both of you niggas got me oh so fucked up! You gon' call me and have me thinking one thing when a move was already made? Are you serious right now?"

The frowns that came across their faces were priceless, so I decided to end the charade with a smile.

"Thank you," I told them. "I didn't need something else to think about."

There was silence, then it was broken by Kyle's laughter.

"I wanted to laugh as soon as you came in railing on them, but I didn't want to kill it!" Kyle said between laughs. "Oh man, their faces dropped like hundred-pound sacks of potatoes!"

D-Wild and Lil Ru looked at each other and then back at me. D-Wild hung his head as Lil Ru approached me with a smile that showed two iced-out fangs in the midst of his pearly whites.

"Ma, you really had the honey going for real," Lil Ru said, opening his arms for a hug. "Give me some fucking love before I really become offended."

I looked at D-Wild, who was looking at me. He gave me

a nod, and I hugged Lil Ru like the long-lost friend that he was. When I pulled away and looked up at him, I hadn't really realized how much I missed his company as a friend.

"It's good to see you, Ru," I told him seriously. "You gon' stay out of trouble long enough to do your best shit this time?"

"I don't want to make no promises until your problem is dealt with first," Lil Ru answered stiffly. "Then we'll look into it after that."

The fire in his eyes spoke of the violence that he had inside him. It was almost as if there was another person inside of him, or it might be the old Ru ready to rear his head. Made me think of when D-Wild gave me the analogy of the business/street nigga.

"Okay," I stated, knowing I could not change his mind.

Resuming my survey of the room, I saw Jazmine with her three homegirls, Egypt, Porsche, and Kash, who she had already introduced us to. King Ross and King Polo were also in the room. The only people that were missing were Cat Daddy and his band of misfits, but I knew the reasoning behind that. It wasn't until Lil Ru's cousin, Dago, came through the glass doors that I knew we were complete in the aspect of having a formidable number of people.

I saw the potential of an organization that was coming together with the ambitions to succeed on a collective goal.

Papi always told me to surround myself with those who are of the same mind. We may not go about things the same way and not always agree with each other's ways. Still, in the end, those differences form a bond, unit, and family that would be unbreakable. Respect builds loyalty and gives you faith in those around you that they will hustle with the same amount of purpose, if not more, as you reach and exceed the standards set. Togetherness and unity are beautiful things when they are done with sincerity and utmost honesty and with no hidden agendas.

Build a power structure for everyone to excel and get money.

****

An hour and a half into everyone becoming acquainted, Cat Daddy's Caprice and Easy Money's Silverado pulled into parking spaces across from the storefront office. I broke away from Kyle and Dago to meet them at the glass doors.

The plan, as it were, was for Easy Money to inform the Carsons that I had contacted him and was aiming to hire him on a contract. He was to make them believe that even though his loyalty was only to the currency paid to him, he had an underlying respect for them and wanted to show his respect by informing them of the situation.

I was hoping that their appearance brought good news or progress.

The way they appeared, you shouldn't even think twice about their statuses in the streets, but it was how they carried themselves that told the story if you were smart enough to read. Cat Daddy was his usual extravagant self, dressed to the nines in a tailored blue suit, gator skin shoes, and fedora to match. Money Mike wore a black pinstriped number with shoes polished to a high shine. Sir Brit also wore an all-black number but opted to ditch the coat and wear a Kangol. Easy Money wore a maroon three-piece custom-fitted suit with matching wing tips. The brother's swag was a definite match for the company he kept.

As I reached the door, Cat Daddy paused the group and looked in my direction as he said something to the rest. I stepped outside in time to catch Sir Brit's comment.

"Let's just take care of them both and be done with it," Sir Brit insisted.

"It ain't part of the plan," Money Mike responded calmly, fixing his cuffs and showing off his dollar-sign-shaped diamond cufflinks. "Besides, we get to have a little fun since we missed out on going to Atlanta."

I rewound back to when I first called Cat Daddy, and he said they were on their way out of town but put it on ice to help me out. I never even asked or considered that they gave up on an undisclosed amount of money, passing up a hustle to stay and deal with this.

"I apologize for that and putting you all in the mix to miss money," I relayed, letting them know that I knew what Money Mike was speaking on.

Though Cat Daddy and Money Mike were twins, their personalities set them apart. On this occasion, it was Money Mike who seized the moment.

"Look here, E, like I told you before, I fuck with you the long way. In no way am I fucked up bout missing a trip to stay here and fuck with you," Money Mike said, walking forward. "You like a little sister to us, and we'll go to bat for you at a moment's notice. When you called Cat Daddy for help, he ain't have to say nothing but that you needed help. And I was on the phone putting all other matters on hold until we got to the bottom of your situation. Which is now our situation as a whole. Now, come here."

Money Mike opened his arms for a hug, and I didn't hesitate to embrace him. His words touched me to no end because, as my teachers, they didn't reveal emotion to distract me from my lessons. When one was complete, it was on to the next without a word of congrats of any kind.

"Understand something, Envy. You been one of us for a long while now, and you a fast learner, so this is a lesson you need to learn. I believe Easy Money expressed his view on it out of Cordova," Money Mike said, still hugging me. "Our words are the most powerful weapons we have, besides our brains, 'cause it's our words that make believers out of people. Go against those words, and no one will take you at your word for fear of disappointment. Do it look like we want to be disappointments on any level and not have people take us at our word?"

"No, the direct opposite," I answered without a second thought.

"Exactly," Money Mike said. "Now, you can let go. I don't want you wrinkling my suit."

I had to laugh because Money Mike was the only one I knew to ever turn a sweet conversation into a comedy in the blink of an eye.

"And you wonder why I always show you love and hug you last," I remarked as I let go and playfully punched him in the arm.

He gave me a wounded look, and I laughed again as he rubbed his arm with a smile on his face.

"I don't mean to kill the mood in any way, but I was informed that you own an escort service," Easy Money said with interest. "Is it on the legal market, along with the strip club that was burned to the ground?"

"Yeah, Diamond Escorts is on the legal market, but not in the phone book like the Diamond House is," I answered. "It was a mixture of the girls that we used for parties. That's how I pulled it off."

"Maybe, when this is over, we can discuss business, and you can educate me on a few things," Easy Money said.

"Seeing as you at the main office right now, after you let me know what happened, we can get into that even in the midst of this situation," I responded, wanting to extend my gratitude. "If you got a business name, we can put it on paper and go from there. My business manager, Kyle, is also a part of this outfit."

With that being said, Easy Money went on to tell me about his meeting with the Carsons. It was initially for Poppa Carson, but he knew Angie would become a part of the meeting. After hearing that I wanted to put a contract on Angie, Poppa Carson became irate and even called Papi in front of Easy Money, giving him the news. The response had not been to his liking because he made an offer to hit both me and Papi.

Easy Money said he politely declined the offer. On his way out the door, he told Poppa Carson and Angie that he chose sides and was locked in with the 220/221 Hustle Mafia

Family. He said that when the door closed, he heard a bunch of yelling and Poppa Carson hollering, "This is your fucking fault!" which caused me to smile.

Cat Daddy said they had talked to Papi before they executed the plan and after when Poppa Carson made an offer to have us hit. So, Papi was on point and most likely had Queen running loose around the yard. He also had Miguel and Uncle B with him and momma. That was when Easy Money told me that he left Smoke with Papi, and Smoke would protect that house with his dying breath. Easy Money and Papi walked both Queen and Smoke around the house, giving Smoke commands throughout, making sure Smoke knew how far to venture from the house. Papi liked to leave the doors open around the house at certain times during the day.

Papi also sent me a message, saying I should play for keeps and don't leave anything of my enemy.

When we finished, we headed inside with the others and introduced Easy Money into the mix. I came to find out that Lil Ru and Easy Money knew each other in passing before Lil Ru got locked up. There was a beef back then that never got settled.

That drew me to pause.

"We going to find out because he inside right now," I said as I turned to the doors to go inside.

I turned to see if they were coming, and they followed me in a purposeful stride. When I reached the doors, Lil Ru stepped out and looked at me.

"I was only waiting for y'all conversation to end before

I made my presence felt if it wasn't already known," Lil Ru said slowly with a blunt in his mouth. "You might want to stay for this."

"Ru!" Easy Money called out behind me.

"Naw, naw, nah, my guy," Lil Ru went around me.

Easy Money broke off the group and met Lil Ru face-to-face halfway.

"You got something you want to tell me, Easy?" Lil Ru asked calmly, eyeing Easy Money.

You could see the size difference since Easy Money was smaller than Lil Ru, who stood at 6'1". You could see the coiled energy in Easy Money that told you that if you come, you better come hard.

"Yeah, I do, my guy," Easy Money replied. "But I don't think you gonna like a word I say."

"How bout if I don't like a word you say, we take care of this the hard way," Lil Ru responded with a shrug.

"Just like I told you before, we came to the agreement that we go our separate ways," Easy Money stated clearly. "You made your bed, so lie in it. You wanted to crash out for a hot dollar that ended up being crumbs to what I had planned for you to take care of."

"The hit was legit!" Lil Ru remarked, throwing the blunt down.

"It was a rush job, and nobody knew where nobody was," Easy Money cut in. "That crew you was with was dumpster juice, sticky shoes, my guy. You said it yourself that you barely knew the handler."

Lil Ru remained silent.

"Then, in the end, somebody snitched you out," Easy Money dropped the final bomb of information. "Yeah, you should've heard me knocking at your door, and Chula answered, telling me the news."

"You coulda hit me up while I was gone, bruh," Lil Ru said, dropping his head. "You know you could have."

"What lesson is it when you award poor performance? I don't know. Do you?" Easy Money shot back. "I said it was supposed to be you and I. Not Tom, Dick, and Harry. I don't trust everybody."

"I should punch you down for not trusting me out of all people," Lil Ru said heatedly. "I ain't give you a reason not to."

"One, I trust you beyond a shadow of a doubt. It's your judgment that eludes my trust 'cause you a hot head," Easy Money said, unnerved. "Two, you know that you can try to punch me down, but it'll only be you trying and me doing."

The look in Easy Money's eyes betrayed the calmness of his voice. Cat Daddy, Money Mike, and Sir Brit gave Easy Money room by stepping off to the side.

Lil Ru moved first, throwing a two-piece that Easy Money must have seen coming because he weaved both punches with all the grace of a professional boxer. Lil Ru pressed forward, throwing punches. All of them weaved until he threw a dummy that led Easy Money's head toward the left hook that came out of nowhere. At the last second, Easy Money seen the haymaker coming and tried to block and dip. Easy Money was rocked, but he snapped back just as fast as he got rocked. Regrouping quickly, he made a move nobody could predict and Lil Ru didn't see coming in a million years. Easy Money swung low, snatching Lil Ru's leg towards him, as he sent a jackhammer punch into his gut, relieving Lil Ru of his breath and doubling him over.

"Jail dulled our senses, Ru," Easy Money said, straightening his suit coat. "Strength without coordination and a sharp mind don't mix. Proper preparation and planning prevents poor performance, and practice is what builds excellence and perfection of one's craft."

We all stood there as Lil Ru got off the ground, catching his breath. I was in the mindset that we lost a member before he was even fully incorporated into the fold; "Which?" was the question.

"Damn, my guy. I forgot how hard you hit for a little nigga," Lil Ru said, standing to his full height. "You still could've fucked with a homey, Easy. Yeah, I slipped up, but you know my position."

"If you think it was Dago taking care of your fam and hitting your account every month, you need to call him up so I can straighten his ass out," Easy Money said, evidently annoyed but calm.

"Oh, he told me," Lil Ru said with a smile. "That's why I ain't come out with my pistol and talked before I swung," he paused and rubbed his stomach. "Should've come out with my pistol for your little ass."

"Then I'd have to explain to Chula why I had to pay for your funeral," Easy Money laughed. "Come here, nigga. I missed you. We got to continue your coaching if you gon' ever get off the street nigga shit."

"Fuck you, bruh!" Lil Ru commented as they dapped and bro hugged.

I looked at Cat Daddy, whose response was to shrug his shoulders.

"Okay, if y'all done holding hands as y'all kiss and make up, I'd like to get everybody acquainted and a complete understanding on where everybody stands," I said with sass. "If that's alright with y'all."

Lil Ru laughed, but it was Easy Money who responded.

"Thank you for letting us get this out the way now," Easy Money said suavely. "Now, if you'll lead the way, Madame, we'll kindly accompany you to our futures."

"Money Mike, Easy Money just jumped ahead of you in greeting," I said with a smile as I headed inside.

"Money to Money, I'm already the black sheep. Now, I don't know what color I am," Money Mike commented behind me.

"If you was ever a sheep, then I must be Mary," I heard Easy Money shoot sarcastically.

To think I might be the only lamb in the wolves' den would ease my mind if it were true. Knowing that I fit into this dysfunction? ...Scary.

CHAPTER FOURTEEN

W hat happened inside of Platinum Services was a quiet yet productive event. It was decided that before I could implement the houses I got as trap spots, I would have to put the Kings Gate Crew in one of them and turn two others into a cash house and stash house. That meant I needed two or three more properties to add to my expenses. While I was outside, everybody who stayed were thinking on the next moves.

Jordan already knew a building for sale to renovate into another Red Carpet Salon, while Kyle and Vanessa were looking into contractors on the rebuilding of Diamond House. Even though D-Wild and I were an item, Dorian made sure business and pleasure didn't mix by fulfilling his role in getting the product he was supposed to distribute. Once Kyle's Kings Gate Crew were loaded to a spot, Dorian, Michael, and Calvin would then choose the stash house. While discussions went on, my mind flipped to the plan of eradicating the Carson problem without facing time for it. I knew Cat Daddy and his group were more than capable. But, for some reason, I felt a message needed to be made so it would be known, but not apparent to the legal system, who got it done and why. Then, it came to me like lightning.

Orange Mound Money Gang. In debt and expendable.

As if feeling the shift in me, Michael broke off from Dorian and Calvin to make his way to me.

"You figured something out," Michael said knowingly.

"Yeah," I responded, still letting it formulate in my head.

"Good," Michael remarked. "Are we gon' like it, though?"

I shrugged my shoulders dismissively in response, knowing I would have to bring my thoughts to the table soon anyway.

Michael's intense eyes took me in like he used to do when he was getting used to me. I didn't flinch, merely waiting.

"Since you got a flair for being dramatic, let me help you out." He finally said, turning his back to me and facing the entire room.

The whistle he gave was loud and long, gaining everyone's attention quickly without a problem.

"Envy came up with something to deal with our particular problem as we know it to be at the moment," he said, then looked over his shoulder at me. "Floor's yours, boss."

I was never good at public speaking, and knowing the role I had and the pressure of it, I was nervous. Dialing every fiber of Boss Bitchness in me, I took a deep breath and said the only thing I knew would come out before there was an uproar.

"Orange Mound Money Gang should do the hit," I stated plainly and waited for the onslaught of shouts to begin.

To my surprise, to my ears came silence in, which I'd never known. The only way I figured that I may even be a little on point in my decision was D-Wild, who walked to a window to look outside.

"I'm not even gon' sugarcoat it, ma," D-Wild said, still looking out the window. "That shit sound crazy as fuck, and even for me, I might add. The same crew that crossed you in the first place and you made a deal with?"

I didn't say a word because it sounded extra crazy when said like that. But my shock came next.

"It's crazy enough to work," D-Wild said, turning towards me. "They in debt, and they want to be in your good graces for riding with snitches that tricked them into riding against you." He paused, still piecing it together like I was. "We need to get hold of DiVinci and Capone ASAP."

"Everything could work out, but it has a downside," Cat Daddy mentioned.

"They could side up with the Carsons and make a deal," I responded, receiving a nod. "That's why we throw the Klan info at them, an incentive of being out of debt and forming a potential truce. We'll still keep an eye on them, though, for moves against us."

"That won't be necessary," Money Mike said, gaining attention. "When they got dropped off, I gave them a proposition of my own."

"Okay, don't keep an asshole in suspense," Cat Daddy responded sarcastically. "Since we all just now hearing this."

"Don't use that tone with me, bruh," Money Mike said, frowning. "I took the initiative because y'all was handling the Carson meeting. When the body moves, the brain is still supposed to operate at full capacity."

Cat Daddy remained silent at the words that struck true.

"Now, I asked the niggas if they would be willing to put in work if it became a necessity and to clear some of the slate so word wouldn't get out they help some snitches," Money Mike said, eying Cat Daddy. "I knew it would work in our favor if it was in there, as a possibility, to be called upon. So, they could right something they unknowingly had a hand in instigating. Seeing as Envy came up with the idea to use them, I'm even more confident I made the right choice." He paused, measuring his words. "As for now telling you, I didn't feel it was important because we could deal with it ourselves, and I was planning on using them as a decoy when we really began coming together on dealing with the Carsons."

I smiled on the inside because this was what I needed around me. Ambition and initiative are qualities needed to be successful in life. Everyone around me were leaders in their own right. Yet, they chose to rally behind and beside me as a focal joint in a point organization. Being able to educate myself with the different minds in my company gave me an advantage no other had. While others used people who only followed and had no voice, I, on the other hand, had an organization of real bonafide bosses who had their own and could move without assistance. The caliber of people around me was so high that if I couldn't learn from them, I shouldn't be in this game we call life.

"Thank you, Money Mike. You just got an extra ten-second hug," I remarked with a smile. "Can you take care of it since you already spoke with them about it?"

"You are very welcome, ma. The hug won't be necessary, though," Money Mike responded seriously, eyeing Cat Daddy. "Now, you, on a side note, bruh, we not gon' get into a conversation over this in front of everybody. So, if you want to go outside and discuss something with me, then we can do that after I make this call for Envy."

In response, Cat Daddy made his way outside while Money Mike made the call to DiVinci and Capone. I went outside to talk to Cat Daddy and hopefully de-escalate the situation between the two. People forget that even though Cat Daddy did most of the talking, him and Money Mike were twins who came up the exact same way. Their temperaments were the same, and it was only because of their little brother, Sir Brit, that the balance between them always leveled out.

As I stepped outside, Cat Daddy's fedora and suit coat were laid across the hood of my car. The concentrated look on his face put me in the mindset that there was going to be a second fight in front of the Platinum Services Office. I had to bring control to the situation and some peace--unless this was how we would deal with disagreements throughout the organization as a whole.

"Before you try to calm things down, allow me to let you in on something very important," Cat Daddy began, not looking at me. "Even though we're brothers, twins at that, I raised all three of us. Money Mike is the oldest, but he didn't want to carry the responsibility of thinking for the three instead of one, so I took lead." He rolled his shoulders like they were heavy.

"After that, we decided on a chain of command. Later on down the line, when we became more sophisticated with our movements, we made mutual agreements." Cat Daddy explained. "No moves were made without discussing them with the rest, and if there was one made, then inform the rest so we can come together in planning for whatever came next. Failure to do so would require a sort of violation. That includes even yours truly."

"There's one thing you failed to mention," Money Mike's voice came from behind me. When I turned to look, I saw he also had his suit coat off. "There's a difference between moves and contingency plans, and that's what I had in mind. How soon we forget the full understanding of each other and the rules set."

"You were supposed to let us in," Cat Daddy argued. "Not keep it to yourself when you had ample opportunity to bring it to the table."

"That's what this is about?" Money Mike questioned. "Cause I ain't tell you? Really? Or is it 'cause I came up with it before you did?"

"You think I'm vain?" Cat Daddy said, offended. "If you woulda brought this out, we could have already had the wheels in motion and implemented it as part of the plan to dethrone the Carsons. Fuck the credit!" He paused and looked at me. "Even Envy is smart enough to know I don't come up with all the ideas. She knows it's a group effort. She only looks to me because that's how we've done it for years before she even knew us."

Listening to them talk, I decided on a course of action to hopefully kill all of this.

"Look, I actually see both of y'all points in the argument. So, I have a suggestion or a favor. However you want to put it," I interrupted the conversation between them. "There is still the situation of coordinating. So, I need y'all to leave this alone and fully focus on that, please. I love y'all like my own brothers, and y'all know I don't have any. This is minor shit for major players and shouldn't come between family. Restructure y'all agreement with Sir Brit and Easy Money and become my advisors. I also need help building an infrastructure with rules, guidelines, protocols, and procedures put in place to eliminate possibilities of failure among our family."

I didn't let them respond as I left them outside. When I passed through the doors, Easy Money and Sir Brit stepped out to join Cat Daddy and Money Mike. To the left of the door was Money Mike's suit coat, which was neatly laid across a chair. I turned to look back outside and saw that all four of them had formed a loose circle and were in deep conversation.

This brought me to a thought that needed to be shared but could wait until later. I'd rather deal with the immediate and leave the rest to make itself into a clever picture. I turned around to face the room.

"Listen up, everybody," I said, getting the room's attention. "Unless they come together on a few things amongst themselves, I want to deal with something else."

When I noticed that I had everyone's undivided attention, I turned back towards the window. This was important, so I knew I needed to use the right words to get my point across.

"We are equals in the grand scheme of things, first and foremost," I continued slowly. "With that said, an organization without structure is destined to crumble because there isn't any foundation to hold it up or a frame to hold it together. Kyle, Kayla, Dorian, and D-Wild are to be my seconds-in-command. Cat Daddy is also, but this conversation is for those in this room." I paused, still watching the conversation outside. "Now, crews will be formed with these people at the lead. Jazmine and Lil Ru, if you choose to be a part of this, you'll have to join a crew. Your respective crews outside of this are yours, but when it comes to this family business, you gon' have to follow somebody. On a personal level, we are on equal ground, but on the business side..." I turned back to face the room. "I am the Boss Bitch. When it comes to the 220/221 Hustle Mafia Family, I am the HBIC. If you want to play dumb, I am the Head Bitch In Charge."

"Look, ma, we already got that overstood on the hierarchy, and who answers to who," Lil Ru said with a smile. "Kyle actually knows you well and insisted we get that understanding before moving forward."

"He also let us know how you been running your business and figured you would want to run this the same way," Jazmine added with a gun. "Seems he knows his Boss Bitch to a 'T.'"

"I also know that you gon' remain in the trenches hustling with the rest of us like the soldier you are," D-Wild spoke up. "The only thing is, we gon' make sure we can keep your hustle in the corporate market while we take care of the other side."

I didn't know how much I was stressing until I felt the tightness leave my shoulders. It felt like a massive weight left me, and I was lighter. Kyle really knew me better than anybody else did, and for him to take things into his own hands, evaluate the situation, and then consider how I would respond made me smile. Kyle hadn't been with me the longest, so I put him on the game as I know it.

D-Wild's statement was the situation that would need to be brought up later because my legit business was already set up and could wash the money in our organization. Everyone had their hustle, but everybody had a dream job they had always wanted. That was where the situation would come. I knew I could negotiate it to benefit, but what I would ask for in return would call for ambition on the other's part. The money Kyle, Kayla, and Dorian's crews would make was already tied to me and was all mine.

"We got a problem," Cat Daddy's voice came from behind me. "And I do mean a problem."

He explained that the Carsons officially put a hit out on Papi and me. He received the call as a professional respect because it was known all around that Cat Daddy and his brothers used to run for Papi and made a pledge in front of a group of contract workers that Papi was off limits, or it would be taken personally. The hit wouldn't be a problem if the contact didn't go through a dude named Savage Life.

When Cat Daddy and his brothers made their pledge for

Papi, it was Savage Life who came forward and told them that even though he respected them, if the hit came his way down the line, he would take it and carry it out. Savage Life was a legend in Memphis, being in his thirties and revered for the way he put in work. Savage Life was a Hispanic dude who could blend in anywhere with anyone.

To be true to his word, Savage Life was the one who called Cat Daddy and informed him of our current problem.

When I asked what advice they had on handling Savage Life, they told me to use the keys Easy Money gave me earlier. Easy Money insisted I ride with him and almost came to blows with D-Wild.

When Easy Money gave me the idea of riding with him, D-Wild told him that if I rode with anybody, it would be with him. I could see the protectiveness that D-Wild was showing and could understand it. It wasn't until Easy Money told him that he could protect me better than D-Wild that shit came to an abrupt halt. A look of absolute anger crossed D-Wild's face. Before anybody could move, D-Wild had his pistol out and was pointing at Easy Money.

"You can't protect her better than me from a grave, my guy," D-Wild's voice came out hard. "I been running a cemetery without a license for years, and I ain't had one complaint to cross my desk."

"D..." I started.

"Nah, Envy. I want to get this understood with the guy over here," D-Wild cut me off. "That means if your name ain't D-Wild or Easy Money, stay out the way." His attention went back to Easy Money, who still hadn't moved. "Now,

Easy Money, if you think you gon' take my baby anywhere out of my sight with shit hitting the fan, then I'll body you here and now."

"Pull the trigger," Easy Money said with a shrug.

"Nigga, you think it's…" D-Wild began, but the smooth movement of Easy Money paused him.

When D-Wild went to respond, Easy Money pulled out a nasty-looking revolver as fast as I had ever seen and pointed it at D-Wild.

"I don't think nothing, my guy," Easy Money said coldly and calmly. "What I know is that you pulled your iron on me and ain't used it yet. The only reason I ain't split your melon is because of Envy, and we suppose to be a team." Easy Money lowered his gun hand and continued, "I'll let that shit slide this one time, and we discuss this like gentlemen. Although, if you want to keep that 40 pointed at me, I can down you before you tighten your finger on that trigger."

"Fuck that!" my voice fueled heatedly because I knew this was going to end one of two ways. "What the fuck we about to do is calm this shit down and discuss this shit like I want discussions to be in here, my guy! Or y'all can walk out the door, and I can take care of my damn self!"

I understood now. The first move was to weed out the ignorant and insignificant bullshit about who didn't have time for the big dick contest.

"We going to solve this like this right now," I continued in a business-like fashion. "If you are going to continue the dramatic theater y'all producing, then leave and go do your own shit with another crew or your own. I'm not going to force my loyalty on anyone. So, when do you two gentlemen want to ride off in the sunset with a Boss Bitch on some suit and tie shit? And, yes, they make 'em in the female fashion as well as the male," I said with a slickness, knowing that a bitch had to put on my big girl thong. "We can be on something bigger. I was well on my own, so the two of you want to disagree. Cool. So, how about three of us disagree?"

"I don't have a problem," Easy Money said, putting away his gun. "He pulled on me. Now, I'm always ready to discuss disagreements as a gentleman and a businessman, but I never pull a firearm on a family member unless I intend to use it."

D-Wild finally put his pistols away, and I saw a new reserve in him, like a new person just grew into him.

"I don't trust many, my guy. Envy is the Queen to my King, and I protect my Queen as a King should," D-Wild said. "I'm here to ride or die through the aftermath of anything situated with her. As her King, I'll take care of mine. If you want to assist, you welcome to by any means because help is always good to have."

A grin crossed Easy Money's face.

"What's funny, my guy?" D-Wild asked, tilting his head in question.

"Nothing at all, pimpin. That was a smile of respect." Easy Money responded, still with a grin. "A man takes care of home and heart with the best of his ability or greater. If you wouldn't have disagreed, I would have thought you was soft. The pistol wasn't necessary."

"You know you two are going to drive me crazy if this gon' be y'all relationship with each other, right?" I said, hoping to completely ease all the tension.

"All relationships with Easy Money are like this," Lil Ru spoke. "Blame it on all those damn books he reads."

"Reading is fundamental to survival, as well as mathematics. If the brain doesn't exercise, then the body becomes a shell. Worthless to human existence," Easy Money schooled Lil Ru. Then he looked back at me. "Now, when we visited earlier today, I insisted I be over your security, and you agreed. So, that's what I'm here for, and I do my job extremely well and professionally." His eyes cut to D-Wild, and he continued. "There was no disrespect intended. I only meant to point out that my assistance could have her completely off-grid, and set her up somewhere safe."

"You know what? Fuck it. It's good, my guy," D-Wild said, holding his hand out to shake Easy Money's.

No words were exchanged as Easy Money grasped D-Wild's hand to shake. This relieved me because now that the craziness was over and I asserted my position and authority, we could move on to more pressing matters.

CHAPTER FIFTEEN

T he next few days were the rockiest I ever had. After refusing to hide out and remaining in plain sight, D-Wild hovered around like a male lion protecting his pride. Easy Money loaded my house down and wired it up with a system so advanced with so many cameras that I felt like I was a government official with high-level clearance. Easy Money left his dog, Smoke, with me after he put in a dog door at the front, garage, and patio doors.

Smoke was welcomed company, and he was well-trained. I asked why he didn't get left with Papi anymore, and I was told with vigor that since I didn't want to be ducked off anywhere, I would need all the protection I could get. Besides, Easy Money was giving Papi the same technology treatment I received. Which put me at ease, knowing we had the same level of competence around both of us.

Sitting on the couch in front of my 75" flat screen, I was still learning the controls and sequences of the cameras when I flipped to the camera for my front yard. Something caught my eye. I didn't recognize the truck that drove into my driveway and parked beside my Lexus.

I reached for the .380 on the coffee table and stood up, eyes still on the screen. I made sure a round was in the chamber and whistled for Smoke. He came in from the backyard, tail wagging.

We got some company, boy," I said aloud.

As if understanding, Smoke's tail stopped wagging, and he sniffed the air. He started to move before I stopped him with a hand motion.

"Wait," I said, focusing back on the truck that still sat in my driveway, but nobody exited.

My phone began to ring with the default tone set for unknown callers. I looked at the phone, then back at the screen of the truck.

I picked the phone up and answered.

"Hello?" I answered, eyes locked on the TV screen.

"You don't know me, Envy, but what I have to say is important nonetheless," the voice said deeply through the phone.

"You got 10 seconds to tell me who this is, or you can talk to D.T.," I responded, annoyed.

"D.T.?"

"Dial Tone, my guy. Now, who is this?" I asked, already taking a wild guess.

There was silence on the line but movement on the TV screen as the truck's driver door finally opened.

"If you must know," came the answer as a man stepped

out of the truck with a phone to his ear. "My name is Savage Life, or Savage for short."

"What a pleasant surprise it is to hear from the man on contract for my life," I responded sarcastically as I sized up the screen. "May I ask the nature of your call?"

He laughed. The man on the screen did the same, confirming that they were one and the same. The dude was dressed in all black but did not cover his head, so I could make out all his features with the sun shining on him.

· "You have wonderful manners, I must say," Savage drawled. "The nature of my call is about the outcome of your health."

I remained silent.

"As I'm guessing, you already know I'm in your driveway," he continued. "Now, any other time, I wouldn't give you the satisfaction of seeing me coming, but we need to talk."

I stayed silent.

"Honestly, I don't like nor respect the Carsons at all, but," Savage paused for emphasis. "I have a reputation. I'm being paid fifty grand for you and Papi, a piece. A hundred grand in total."

I was still silent because I didn't want to jump to conclusions and wanted him to say it himself.

"I've got a business proposition for you to get me out of your hair," he said. I watched on the screen as he leaned on his truck. "I already have the money from the Carsons, but for that same hundred grand plus fifty, I'll forget about you and take care of them KKK motherfuckers."

"How bout you take they money and just say they paid

for their own hits?" I asked, flicking through the cameras around the house until I was back to Savage. "That way, you can call it even."

"You know, Cat Daddy told me the same thing you just did. Not in the same way, but close enough," Savage said with a sigh. "I'm actually impressed. You seem so calm and under control. So, this is what I'll do."

On the screen, he pushed off of his truck and looked at my house before moving. He disappeared off-screen, and I flipped through the screens before I found him at my front door.

"Can you see me?" he asked.

"Why?" I asked, keeping my voice level.

"Keep looking."

He removed his shirt and turned in a slow circle with hands above his head. He then took his shoes off and knocked them together. After that, he raised his pants legs one at a time. The phone went back to his ear.

"I'm unarmed, and I bet you not. Plus, you got a dog that been running around," Savage said. "Let me in so we can talk face-to-face and come to an understanding."

Dude must've thought I was a dingy bitch with no snap at all. At the same time, I changed my mind.

"Stay there," I said, then hung up and watched the screen. I dialed Cat Daddy, and he answered on the third ring.

"Yeah," he answered.

"Guess who's at my front door," I remarked.

"I'm on my way," Cat Daddy responded. "I'm twenty minutes away from you."

"The front door will be unlocked," I responded and ended the call.

I looked at Smoke, who hadn't moved since I called for him.

"Watch 'em, and be ready to kill," I commanded as I headed to the door with Smoke on my heels.

With .380 in my right hand, I opened the door with my left.

Savage stood there. He was about 5'8' on the slim side, but you could see where his strength lay. He was well-proportioned with slim muscles and not ugly at all. He gave you the impression of Tyrese from Fast and Furious, but he was dripping with swag, so intoxicating it came off of him in waves. Smoke must have sensed the shift because he began to growl low and deep.

I stepped out of the way, allowing him entrance. He looked at my gun hand and smiled, revealing an iced-out grill before taking a step. I closed the door when he was all the way in and had the thought to end him right there.

"Stop right there," I instructed, pointing my pistol at him. "Don't even turn around. Strip down to your boxers, head to the couch, and have a seat."

Savage complied without argument and got undressed until he had on nothing but socks and boxers. After stripping, he moved on ahead towards the living room. I gathered his clothes and followed behind him with Smoke by my side, still growling. He took a seat on the couch in the middle seat. I came around and sat in the chair off to the right of him.

"Watch 'em, Smoke," I commanded, and Smoke locked

onto Savage with another growl.

I proceeded to search Savage's clothes for concealed weapons. I only found his wallet, phone, and keys, which read Nissan. In his shoes, I didn't find anything either. I tossed him his clothes but kept the shoes. Then I had a thought.

"Take off your socks," I commanded since I knew niggas who kept a lot of shit in their socks because when cops searched you, they rarely checked the socks.

He sat the clothes next to him without a word and took his socks off one after the other. He must have known what I was after because he peeled them off and let them roll inside out, then lifted his feet.

"You can get dressed now," I said, tapping the pistol on my knee and wondering why he was being so cooperative. "Tell me why I shouldn't shoot you and be done with it."

Savage finished getting dressed before looking at me like a predator scenting prey. My eye contact didn't waver because I wanted him to see I wasn't his typical prey and would drop him sure as shit stank. He came to a conclusion and smiled again.

"Two reasons why you shouldn't kill me," he said, leaning back. "One, I came here not looking to harm you, or you wouldn't have seen me coming no matter what you did. Second, and most importantly, professionalism."

I remained silent, still tapping my knee with the pistol.

"Besides, doing me won't stop the Carsons' hit on you and Papi," he continued. "As long as I got the contract, you're safe. For now. That is if we can come to a mutual business understanding." He continued, "I did my digging on you when I got the contract. I didn't even know Papi had a daughter, so imagine my surprise when I found out. So, I derived a plan and course of action that could possibly benefit all parties except for the Carsons."

I let my silence forward him on.

"Word through the wire is that the Carsons are long-standing members of the Klan. I did my research on that as well." He paused for effect, "Now, I could take their money and give them a one-finger salute, sure enough. On the flip side of that, I would lose clientele because people would feel my word has less value."

Hearing enough and figuring where the conversation was going, I held my hand up to stop him.

"Savage, you insult me and my gangsta," I said loudly. "First, you come out saying you want a hundred grand plus fifty. Then you come into my home after accepting a contract on me." I looked at the TV screen because movement caught my eye. "See, where I'm from, we call that extortion. If you came here after you took the Carsons off the board, I would be more accepting of your proposition." My front door opened, and four people entered through it. I stood to my feet. "So, you need to hope that these gentlemen coming in have more interest in it than I do."

Savage's eyes shifted, and I could see the uncertainty in his eyes about his decision to approach me, but it was too late.

Easy Money whistled and gave Smoke the command to go outside, and the dog walked off, looking back every few steps at Savage.

"Savage Life," Cat Daddy said.

"Cat Daddy," Savage responded.

"Damn, Savage, you had to take the contract, didn't you?" Money Mike said heatedly while Sir Brit lingered in the background, out of sight of Savage.

"I told y'all I would if it came to me," Savage answered. "The only thing is that I could've carried the hit out already but haven't. Y'all know me for my work, so think on that."

"Well, that is true, but it doesn't excuse the fact that I informed the people of our tradecraft that I would take it personal on whoever took the job," Cat Daddy said, sitting on the couch next to Savage. "By you being a vet, you should know and understand that words are more than letters fit together at random."

"Exactly, which is why I took the job. Because I said I would," Savage agreed. "The thing is, I never said what I would do with it."

This drew a pause from Cat Daddy, getting a reaction from me.

"So, I'm supposed to be the damsel that's happy you took the job but had an ulterior motive?" I ask sarcastically.

His silence pissed me off, and I pointed my pistol at him.

"Hold on, Envy," Cat Daddy said. "If he don't answer these next two questions correctly, we gon' turn him to Casper."

I didn't say anything but kept my pistol pointing at Savage.

"Say, Easy Money, you thinking what I'm thinking?" Cat Daddy asked, looking at Savage.

Easy Money pulled a pistol from his waist and cocked it.

"One question only," Easy Money stated calmly.

"Savage Life, you heard it for yourself, and we are all in agreement that you only get one shot at this. No pun intended," Cat Daddy said, standing up. "Let your answer be that of your true feeling, not what you believe we want to hear, please."

"Done," Savage replied with renewed steel to his voice, accepting the situation for what it was.

****

By being an old head in the game, Savage knew his options were limited, but you can't deny his gangster by a long shot. Cat Daddy asked one simple question that really wasn't simple.

Did he want to live?

His response was classic and full of game, about life meant to be free without bounds. So, to live was a state of being that most took for granted, not understanding the purpose of living.

Instead of ending there, Cat Daddy asked a second question, and I sensed that Savage's response was satisfactory to him. It was Savage's answer to the second question that fucked me up and had me thinking. The fact of the matter was that he didn't really take the hit but received the info about it. After finding out that Papi had a daughter, he thought about his own daughter and what he would do to anyone who threatened a hair in her head. Before Savage came to me, he took out Poppa Carson but let Angie live.

An hour later, we were still in my living room but with more company and my pistol put up.

D-Wild picked up Papi and brought him, Uncle E, and Miguel with him. We sat around trying to figure out the significance of the situation at hand because now, Angie being the only child, she could merge Carson City Cartel and the Carson Family Mob together and reign supreme. She would have to get her house in order before she could make any more moves, which was the only plus.

"Cat Daddy, can you get Carson on the phone so I can talk to her?" I asked, thinking forward.

"I'll see what I can do," Cat Daddy responded, reaching into his pocket and leaving the room.

I needed to get my organization together and structure to the point where it appeared it was established as long as Santiago Cartel. The call to Angie would either be a curse or a blessing, depending on how the conversation went.

If there was one.

When Papi got all the info, he asked me what I would do. I could tell that he had come up with a plan of action halfway through being told what was going on. I could go after Angie, but it wouldn't solve my problem because then somebody else would take her place and keep coming.

The conversation from days ago came to mind as I thought on how to proceed.

Before I could go into deeper thought, Cat Daddy returned to the room with his phone still to his ear. I thought maybe he didn't get through until he reached me and gave me the phone.

"Angie," he let me know who was on the line.

This would send things into motion and allow me to become a better analyst of the situation.

"Angie, I won't take much of your time. So, I'll get right into it," I begin skipping the bullshit. "I just received word about Poppa Carson, and I want to say I'm sorry about your loss."

"Envy, let me say this," Angie said with fierce. "Once I lay my father to rest and get the family business in order, you are as good as dead."

I remained silent, wanting her to get it out of her system.

"That fucking wetback Savage Life is first on my list of things to do, and you running a neck-and-neck race with him," she continued. "If you got word that my pops got done hours after it happened, that means you got it from the source. Word to the wise, even though you're not, run and hide 'cause you won't get a chance to enjoy life here in Memphis."

The threat pissed me off because I was not the one that started the beef between us. If anything, I tried to solve the issue like a grown woman. So, it was time to let this bitch have it.

"First of all, it was you who inserted yourself into my business. Secondly, it's your own fault your pops is at Heaven's door waiting on access," I said heatedly, knowing that I was pushing her. "Now, we can easily solve all this with a winner-take-all, but I know you ain't nothing but a little girl playing a grown woman's game. I'll gladly meet you one-on-one anytime, anywhere," I paused, then continued. "Know what? Fuck it. I was going to try and be the bigger woman about all of this, but since you won't let me..."

I looked at Cat Daddy, and he gave me a nod of approval.

"So, if anyone from your mob so much as gets seen anywhere in Oakhaven, no, pass the highway that splits Blackhaven from Oakhaven, it will be seen as an act of war, and you won't get time to mourn your pops," I said, making up my mind to take this shit up a level. "I don't have any say over Blackhaven or Graceland, so you got to take that up with Magic of the Blackhaven Gorillas and the other sets over there. As far as I'm concerned, Hustle Mafia Family is a business enterprise and organization that don't have anything to do with the Carsons as a whole."

I waited for a response from Angie and was rewarded, but not with the response I was looking for. Instead of silence, her action was immediate.

"Enjoy yourself while it lasts because I'm going to bring you off of your high horse and stomp you into the ground," Angie said calmly. "You believe you won and can't be touched. So, I'll correct your perception on the situation."

I decided to put the conversation on speakerphone and Bluetooth it to my stereo system so everyone could hear it.

"You threaten me like I'm supposed to be frightened or something when we both know that I'm not," Angie's voice came over the sound system. "You fail to understand and realize a very vital fact about the situation between us."

"Yeah? That would be?" I asked, unfazed.

"You just now entering the game where I've been in this life for a long minute now. So, I'll leave all the talking to you and deliver the action like I've always done. With that said, don't get comfortable in your newly appointed position there, Envy," Angie stated and ended the call and conversation.

****

The dice we roll for the life we live is always a gamble. Prices are to be paid in order to claim status and bragging rights. Whatever the reason for a person's choices in life, the effort and contribution must match the noise. Backing up your words is important. I don't just claim to be a Boss Bitch, I am a Boss Bitch.

Nobody's future is guaranteed or promised, so to believe a life is ready-made is arrogance. Hustle and hard work, along with dedication and diligence, will prove a person's seriousness to survive and succeed in a lifestyle of their choosing.

Angie doesn't know or understand that my mentality is already set to go hard or die trying.

She is about to find out, as well as the rest of the city, that a Boss Bitch has emerged as a new player in the game.

To Be Continued in
**ENVY: THE DICE WE ROLL
BOSS BITCH CHRONICLES: VOLUME TWO**

ABOUT
THE
AUTHOR

Infamous Brown was born in Houston, TX, and raised in Memphis, TN. He has always had a love for writing, even at an early age. Poems, short stories, and music became the focus. When Infamous was sentenced to 30 years in a Texas Correctional Facility for a crime he was falsely accused of, his writing evolved from a hobby to a method of survival. While incarcerated, Infamous has written numerous novels and dreams of one day walking into a bookstore to find his work on a shelf. Until that day, he continues to write and share his gift with the world from which he was unjustly isolated.

www.ingramcontent.com/pod-product-compliance
Lightning Source LLC
Chambersburg PA
CBHW030322020726
47493CB00004B/1125